ZINK

OTHER YEARLING BOOKS YOU WILL ENJOY:

THE MERMAN, *Dick King-Smith*
FLYING SOLO, *Ralph Fletcher*
THE COOKIE COMPANY, *Ross Venokur*
ON MY HONOR, *Marion Dane Bauer*
AN EARLY WINTER, *Marion Dane Bauer*
MY LOUISIANA SKY, *Kimberly Willis Holt*
SKELLIG, *David Almond*
BABY, *Patricia MacLachlan*
IN THE SHADE OF THE NÍSPERO TREE, *Carmen T. Bernier-Grand*
SEESAW GIRL, *Linda Sue Park*

YEARLING BOOKS are designed especially to entertain and enlighten young people. Patricia Reilly Giff, consultant to this series, received her bachelor's degree from Marymount College and a master's degree in history from St. John's University. She holds a Professional Diploma in Reading and a Doctorate of Humane Letters from Hofstra University. She was a teacher and reading consultant for many years, and is the author of numerous books for young readers.

Cherie Bennett

ZINK

A YEARLING BOOK

Published by
Dell Yearling
an imprint of
Random House Children's Books
a division of Random House, Inc.
1540 Broadway
New York, New York 10036

Visit us on the Web! www.randomhouse.com/kids

Educators and librarians, for a variety of teaching tools, visit us at
www.randomhouse.com/teachers

ISBN: 0-440-22810-7

Reprinted by arrangement with Delacorte Press

Printed in the United States of America

March 2001

10 9 8 7 6 5 4 3 2 1

OPM

Acknowledgments

In 1982, a girl named Kelly Weil was born. In 1991, she was diagnosed with cancer. Two years later, despite spectacular advances in childhood cancer treatment, she was dead.

A few months before her death, Kelly wrote a one-page story about a polka-dotted zebra named Zink. After Kelly's death, her father, Les Weil, created the Zink the Zebra Foundation* in her memory, devoted to celebrating differences and promoting diversity in every form. The foundation's remarkable Zink diversity curriculum is now used by many schools across America.

The Zink the Zebra Foundation underwrote First Stage Milwaukee's commission of my play for young audiences *Zink: The Myth, The Legend, The Zebra* (Dramatic Publishing Company, 1998), premiered by First Stage Milwaukee at Milwaukee's Marcus Center for the Performing Arts under the direction of Rob Goodman in November 1997.

My many conversations with Les Weil; his wife, Jodi Peck; foundation executive vice president Bob Riches; and the extraordinary Rob Goodman helped this project immeasurably.

I also owe great thanks to Dr. Robert Kliegman, chair of

*Readers and educators can contact the Zink the Zebra Foundation at 5150 North Port Washington Road, Ste. 151, Milwaukee, WI 53217, (414) 963-4484.

the Department of Pediatrics at the Children's Hospital of Wisconsin, Medical College of Wisconsin, and the CHW/MCW staff. Pediatric oncologist Dr. Bruce Camitta, to whom Dr. Kliegman referred me and who wrote the afterword to this novel, has been a great resource as well. Thanks also on the medical front to Dr. Peter Gottesfeld, Dr. John Sergent, the pediatric oncology unit of Vanderbilt University (Nashville) Children's Hospital, and pharmacist Abigail Halloran. Great help was also provided by Alan Mzengi, cultural attaché at the Tanzanian Embassy in Washington, D.C.; Tanzanian nationals Drs. Donath Mrawira and Hassan Ali (with the Swahili glossary); Jim Doherty, general curator at the Bronx Zoo; and the Nashville Public Library. Professor Fletcher Moon at the Brown-Daniel Library at Tennessee State University and Paula Covington at the University Library at Vanderbilt University both went out of their way to assist me. Gareth Stevens Publishing in Milwaukee published Kelly's original Zink the Zebra story as a picture book. The translation of Shaaban Robert's poetry is by Professor Clement Ndulute.

The artwork in Zink was created by young people who are either currently battling, in remission from, or cured of cancer. Their names and biographies can be found after the afterword. The following people and organizations helped find many of the young people to do the drawings: Toni Cabat, Chai Lifeline (New York City); Christy Andrews, Children's Wish Foundation International (Atlanta); Jaime Reich, Cancer Cured Kids (East Hills, New York); Jenny Lewis, Vanderbilt University Children's Hospital (Nashville); Dr. Bruce Camitta, Children's Hospital of Wisconsin (Milwaukee).

Helpful feedback was offered by adults and young adults who read early drafts of Zink: Jack Cole, Michelle Collins, Debbie

Sandwith, Kate Emburg, Victoria Elliott, Maia Gottesfeld, and Kat Farmer.

My profound thanks to everyone at Delacorte Press. Craig Virden, Beverly Horowitz, Kevin Jones, Judith Haut, Kathy Dunn, and Lisa McClatchy are the best, and my wonderful, insightful editor, Wendy Loggia, is a blessing. Diana Donovan is an ace copy editor. I am very grateful to my agent, Laura Peterson, at Curtis Brown Ltd., and to Dramatic Publishing Company, publisher of the acting edition of *Zink*.

Finally, I want to single out three more people—one adult and two young adults.

Anyone who has ever worked with me and my husband, Jeff Gottesfeld, knows how closely our work is linked and how our artistic minds are melded. He was dramaturg for the stage version of this story. Every word of every draft of every project goes through him. *Zink* the novel was no exception.

And now, the young adults.

I've made it a point for years to answer personally all my mail from readers—more than twelve thousand letters in eight years. One of these letters, from a girl in Illinois, has led to a treasured friendship. I owe an enormous debt to Alicia O'Brien, now thirteen, who has courageously shared with me the most intimate and sometimes brutal details of her continuing struggle with cancer.

And then there is Kelly, of blessed memory, who has touched more lives more profoundly since her death than I could ever hope to touch in my lifetime. Although we never met, I know she was watching over my shoulder as I wrote, and I pray with all my heart that she is satisfied with my efforts.

Cherie Bennett
FEBRUARY 1999

ZINK

PROLOGUE

Africa

SHLEP EAGERLY BIT the tender head from the succulent termite and chewed it happily.

Life was good. After he'd been hungry for so many months, the terrible East African dry season had finally ended, and the rains had brought him a wonderful variety of things to eat. No longer did the sandstorms pelt everything, including Shlep, with noxious grit.

Best of all, the rains meant the sweat bees were gone. Shlep really disliked those sweat bees. Especially Rhonda, the biggest, loudest, nastiest sweat bee of all. Not only did Rhonda and her band of bees get into Shlep's eyes and under his tail during the dry season, they buzzed nasty gossip all over the savanna.

Buzzzzz. "Did you hear? Ice Z kicked Papa Zeke out of his zebra herd because the old zebra can't keep up!"

Buzzzzz. "Did you see how fat Hiccup the warthog got? She's such a pig that she ate every single tuber she dug up and starved her own babies!"

And oh, how they buzzed about Shlep.

"They say Nature doesn't err," Rhonda would tell any animal who would listen. "But, my dear, surely Shlep the monkey is Nature's mistake because Shlep was born . . . *green*. Green fur, bright as new grass. Tufts of it, can you imagine?"

"No," the listening animal would say with a shudder.

"Yes," Rhonda would buzz. "And he sheds! Every day, more fur on the tree limbs and less on him. Why, soon Shlep will be entirely bald."

Just when the dik-dik or the impala was ready to lope away toward what remained of the nearest watering hole (Rhonda would always sense when she might be losing her audience) the big sweat bee would rush on dramatically.

"But wait, that isn't the strangest thing about Shlep the monkey, my dear. The strangest thing is—well, I might as well come right out and say it—he thinks he's a *zebra*."

"No!" the animal would exclaim.

"Yes. A *z-e-b-r-a,*" she'd spell emphatically, "part of

Ice Z's herd. Have you ever heard anything so ridiculous?"

This tidbit never failed to make the animal laugh, which was exactly when Rhonda would strike. She'd flit into its open mouth or onto an eye to pick up some bit of moisture—this had been her goal all along. By the time the annoyed animal tried to brush Rhonda away, she and the other bees would already have buzzed on to their next target.

There was only one difference between Rhonda's gossip about Shlep and her gossip about all the other animals.

Her gossip about Shlep was true.

GRAZING AT THE BASE of Shlep's baobab tree were the powerful stallion Ice Z and his family herd of twenty zebras. As lead stallion, in charge of his herd's safety, Ice Z did more watching than grazing. Though predators rarely attacked during the day, he was ever vigilant.

Ice Z had once led a small band of bachelor zebras. Usually when a bachelor zebra wants a family herd of his own, he has to woo a mare away from an established family herd by fighting and defeating that herd's lead stallion.

But the year before, Ice Z and his bachelor band had

come upon a family herd whose lead stallion had just been killed by lions. Though zebras fall to predators all the time, it's rare for the lead stallion to be taken down, and this herd was leaderless, lost, and confused.

Now, any ordinary zebra stallion would have eagerly abandoned his bachelor brothers to claim leadership of this family herd.

But Ice Z was no ordinary zebra stallion.

Instead, after he'd established himself as the family herd's new leader, he'd invited all his brother bachelors—even the utterly obnoxious Zilch—to join them. Then he did something even more amazing.

It had to do with Papa Zeke.

Papa Zeke was the oldest and wisest zebra in all of Africa. His own lead stallion days were long behind him, and most zebras on the savanna considered him useless. Not Ice Z. Ice Z tracked down Papa Zeke and asked for the honor of having Papa Zeke join his new family herd.

Then Ice Z declared Papa Zeke the herd's spiritual leader.

Spiritual leader? No one was quite sure what that meant. It was all so peculiar that the sweat bees buzzed about it during the entire dry season.

* * *

HIGH UP IN THE TREE, Shlep scrutinized the savanna, imagining that, like Ice Z, he was responsible for keeping watch over the herd. He was proud that he could tell all the zebras apart. No two zebras had the same stripes, just as no two had the same personality. They were all, however, black and white and four-hoofed. Except him.

There was Zuzi, a pretty, vain filly with narrow stripes near her rump and very long eyelashes. Shlep thought she was silly.

There were the rambunctious, almost-but-not-quite-identical twin mares, Zip and Zap, who were Ice Z's best friends. Zip was smarter, but Shlep thought Zap was nicer.

There was Zilch, whom no mare could stand, which was why he was still a bachelor. Shlep couldn't stand him either. Always perfectly clean, Zilch claimed to be allergic to dust. Usually he lolled in the shade while Zero, a colt who worshiped him, fanned Zilch with his tail.

And there was the formidable Xerxes. Xerxes had a jagged scar on his neck from when he had survived a lion attack. That he had lived to tell the tale made him both respected and feared. He was the type of zebra who would be nice to you one minute and kick you in the side the next.

Shlep worried a lot that Xerxes was ready to challenge Ice Z for leadership of the herd. That scared

Shlep. Xerxes was strong like Ice Z, but he wasn't kind like Ice Z.

While Shlep looked on, Zip and Zap played hide-and-seek in the tall grass, barking playfully. This bark was softer than the one they made when danger was near. It sounded something like "Kwa-kwa."

Shlep jumped off a tree branch, caught himself by the tail, and hung upside down, rocking, above the zebras. "Kwa-kwa!" he cried, imitating them.

Papa Zeke had joined Xerxes and Zuzi to graze under the tree. He looked up at Shlep, a bit of star grass still hanging from his lips.

"Hello, Shlepper," Papa Zeke said. "How's life?"

"Kwa-kwa!" Shlep cried in his best zebra voice.

"Monkeys don't say 'kwa,' Shlep."

Shlep lowered himself further, so that his upside-down head was level with Papa Zeke's nose. "I'm a zebra!" he insisted, as he had a thousand times before.

"You're a monkey, Shlep."

"A *green* monkey," Xerxes added with a sneer.

"Green is very nice," Papa Zeke said. "Some of my favorite things are green." He ducked his head to bite off a particularly delicious bunch of green grass.

"Careful, Papa Zeke," Zip called as she galloped by with Zap in playful pursuit. "Remember how your stomach gets when you eat too much."

"Gas that could bring down a pride of lions at fifty paces," Zilch commented nastily from where he was lolling in the shade.

"Watch the wise remarks, mister," Papa Zeke warned. He shook his head and sighed. "Getting old is no fun, my zebra children. However, it beats the alternative."

Shlep's heart pounded out a hopeful tattoo as he pulled himself back onto the branch. Hadn't Papa Zeke looked *right at him* just now when he'd said "my zebra children"?

"Papa Zeke, can we have storytelling tonight?" Zuzi begged. "Please pretty please with a raindrop on it?"

"Yeah." Shlep nodded eagerly. "All us zebras want a story tonight."

Papa Zeke shrugged. "If Ice Z is on watch and he says it's okay, then all right, okay, a definite maybe."

"Right, Ice Z decides everything," Xerxes agreed. But there was a mean edge to his voice.

"Zink, Zink!" Zuzi cried, prancing excitedly in a circle. "Tell us the Zink story tonight. Was Zink as pretty as me, Papa Zeke?"

"Oh, *puh-lease*," Zilch groaned, exaggerating each syllable. "Hiccup the warthog is prettier than you."

"Is not," Zuzi insisted.

"Is too," Zilch replied.

"Is not."

"Is too."

Zuzi stuck her long tongue out at Zilch. "You stink. Everyone hates you."

"Everyone adores me."

"Kwa," Shlep called tentatively. "Kwa?"

"Zilch, you're such a—" Zuzi began.

"*Kwa-kwa!*" Much louder and sharper. And not from Shlep this time.

It had come from Ice Z.

"Predators!" the herd cried. Xerxes bared his teeth ferociously as Zip and Zap sniffed out the scent of the attackers.

Lions. Six of them, approaching head-on in a rare daylight frontal assault.

"Everyone run with the herd!" Ice Z commanded.

Safe in his tree, Shlep screeched monkey noises as the herd bolted, stronger zebras on the outside, younger and weaker ones in the protected center. Ice Z brought up the rear to be sure all his zebras were safely in front of him.

Suddenly Zilch dashed to the front of the pack, where it was safest. Little Zero tried but couldn't keep up with him. Panicked, Zero turned left as the herd turned right.

This was a calamitous mistake. The attacking lions

shifted their charge and rushed toward the defenseless young zebra.

"Kwa! Kwa!" Zero cried pitifully, running as fast as his spindly legs could carry him. But his puny voice was lost in the din of thundering hooves and roaring lions.

"Kwa! Kwa!" Shlep screeched from his tree branch, hoping the herd would realize Zero's plight. He jumped up and down and tore out tufts of green fur in anguish.

The lions were almost on the small zebra now.

It was too awful to watch. Shlep covered his eyes with his paws. He knew that when the first lioness reached Zero, she'd take a flying leap and snap her powerful jaws down on Zero's defenseless neck.

If that didn't kill him instantly, Shlep knew what would happen next: Zero would continue to cry out.

And the lions would devour him alive.

CHAPTER ONE

Africa Day

THE FOOTBALL FIELD at Briarly Middle School was ablaze with color. One hundred forty sixth-graders, all in traditional African dress, were scattered in groups around the sun-dappled field. Beads danced brightly in the girls' braided hair, and the scary animal masks most of the boys wore seemed almost alive.

Becky Zaslow sat cross-legged in the bleachers, just below a huge banner that read AFRICA DAY: SEPTEMBER 28. Her class was watching Mrs. Hudson, their language arts teacher, cook *ugali,* the Tanzanian national dish, and some spicy bean stew over an open fire in a pit dug into the field. Mrs. Hudson had been born and raised in Tanzania, in East Africa, and she'd explained that *ugali*—a stiff porridge made from ground corn and water—was eaten at almost every meal. The spicy stew came from a recipe her grandmother had taught her.

Becky looked around the football field, where African games, arts and crafts, storytelling, and tribal medicine demonstrations were under way.

Today was the grand finale of their first long study cycle, which had concentrated on Africa. Briarly was on the total immersion method. In math, Becky had used cutouts of African nations to study geometry. In music, she'd learned to sing Swahili songs and to play different African instruments.

But her favorite thing had been working with Ms. Flinn, the art teacher, Mr. Izbecki, the science teacher, and Dr. Keino, an African ecologist from the state university to create a huge scale model of the Serengeti National Park in Tanzania. That model now covered the center of the football field.

They'd fashioned grassy savanna plains from AstroTurf, carved baobab and acacia trees from wood, and painted aluminum foil brownish gray for the muddy Mara River.

But the best part had been making the animals. They'd molded clay to create animals that were indigenous ("native to a country or climate"—the word had been on her last vocabulary test) and painted zebras, lions, warthogs, wildebeests, even a strange antelope called a dik-dik. Hundreds of species lived on the Serengeti, and the model had representatives of most of them.

Before the sixth-graders had begun their work, Mr. Izbecki had shown a film about the Serengeti zebra migration. Thousands of herds of zebras instinctively followed a seven-hundred-mile route in search of grass and fresh water, only to end up nine months later right back where they'd started. All during the perilous journey, the plant-eating (herbivorous) zebras were stalked, attacked, and eaten by meat-eating (carnivorous) predators like lions and leopards.

"The laws of nature seem brutal sometimes," Mrs. Hudson said with the tiniest trace of a Tanzanian accent as she stirred the stew. "I once saw a pride of lions eating a young zebra they'd just taken down. Hyenas waited to pick at the bones, and so many vultures circled overhead that they blotted out the sun."

Becky shuddered and looked at the zebra herds on the scale model. They gleamed in the afternoon sun.

"But the parts make a whole that works," Mrs. Hudson went on. "For example, the predators usually take down the weakest zebras, so the animals don't overpopulate and starve to death. Stronger zebras survive to reproduce, you see?"

No, I don't see, Becky thought. *Why should* any *zebras have to die?*

"So, while I cook, we'll review some things that will be on your exam tomorrow," Mrs. Hudson said.

A few rows away from Becky, Brian Green made a face. A lot of kids didn't like Mrs. Hudson because she was strict and formal with her students. But Mrs. Hudson said her teachers in Tanzania had been the same way with her, and she always spoke of them with reverence.

"Who can define *migrate?*" Mrs. Hudson asked.

To pass from one region or climate to another for feeding or breeding, Becky thought, but her hand didn't go into the air as some others did. Mrs. Hudson called on Channa Gold, who got it right. Channa was the only other kid in the class besides Becky who got straight A's.

"And the name of Tanzania's most famous poet?" Mrs. Hudson asked.

"Shaaban Robert," Channa answered.

The teacher nodded. "Excellent. Let's review a little Swahili. Micah, the meaning of *mimi ni mwalimu?*"

I am a student, Becky thought.

"I am a teacher," Micah answered.

Mrs. Hudson nodded. "Correct."

Becky reddened as if she'd said the wrong answer aloud.

13

"And how does one say *zebra* in Swahili? Becky?"

Everyone turned to look at her.

"Punda pilia?" Becky ventured nervously.

"No, it's *punda milia*," Ashley Chaffin corrected loudly. Her smug gaze fell on Becky.

"I'm sorry," Becky said quickly.

"Correct answer, Ashley," Mrs. Hudson said, "but please raise your hand next time."

Ashley was the prettiest, most popular girl in the entire sixth grade. And she had the most power. Becky felt Ashley's predatory eyes still on her. *She takes down weak kids just like lions take down zebras,* Becky realized.

Ashley was one of the reasons Becky kept her mouth shut most of the time. If you didn't say anything, Becky reasoned, you couldn't say the wrong thing. Middle school was so much more treacherous than elementary school. Say the wrong thing, do the wrong thing, even wear the wrong thing, and your life could be over, just like that.

That was why Becky had agonized before finally picking her Africa Day outfit. She'd made a colorful wrap dress (a *kanga* in Swahili), and her notoriously strict mother had even allowed her some clear lip gloss. Her little brother, Lee, said the dress looked like the living room drapes and her lips looked slimy, so Mrs. Zaslow had sent him out of the room. Then she'd braided and beaded Becky's beautiful long brown hair and given her eight metal bracelets to wear on her wrist.

That morning, after she'd dressed, Becky had stood in front of her parents' full-length mirror, assessing her transformation. Pale and skinny. So *ordinary* looking. Nothing like beautiful Ashley Chaffin. Still, she decided, no girl in a *kanga* she'd made herself, with bracelets on her arms and beads in her hair, could look entirely ordinary. Not even Becky Zaslow.

She'd written about it in her secret journal right before she left for school.

September 28

Today I am an African princess. I feel different.

She'd kept the journal since her parents had given it to her last December for Chanukah. Sometimes, like when she was really sad or angry, she'd write a lot. Other times she'd forget to write for days. And though she'd promised herself to write only the truth, writing only the truth had turned out to be a lot harder than it sounded.

* * *

As Mrs. Hudson sprinkled still more spices into the stew, Becky drew her knees up to her chin and made a vow: *I'm writing the truth about how sick I feel.*

She'd been tired and achy for so long that she couldn't even remember when it had started. She was never hungry. When she'd put on her *kanga,* she'd noticed bruises on her legs, but she figured they were from when Lee had kicked her while showing off his latest superhero moves.

Writing in her journal about feeling sick would somehow make it true. Then she'd have to tell her mother, which would make it really, *really* true. Then her mother would make her go to the doctor. And *then* she'd have to stay home from school until she was better. But middle school wasn't like grade school. You couldn't be absent for days and still get all A's.

No. She simply could not be sick.

"Mrs. Hudson, when's the *ugali* gonna be done?" Brian Green called out. "I'm starving."

" 'Patience is the key to all good things,' " Mrs. Hudson quoted. "That expression is from Ethiopia."

Ashley's hand shot skyward.

"Yes, Ashley?"

"Will that be on our test tomorrow? Because we

don't have our notebooks to write it down, so it wouldn't be fair."

"Consider it a gift, Ashley."

"Thank you, Mrs. Hudson."

The aroma of the spicy stew wafted toward Becky. It made her stomach turn, but she closed her eyes and willed the feeling away. *I will not be sick, I will not be sick,* she told herself. There. The nausea had passed. She opened her eyes and found her teacher looking at her.

"Would you like to be my taster, Becky?" Mrs. Hudson held out a wooden spoon full of *ugali* and hot stew.

Becky shook her head quickly, hoping her teacher wouldn't be mad. She hated for anyone to be mad at her, especially Mrs. Hudson. Becky didn't dislike her the way the other kids did. In fact, Mrs. Hudson was Becky's favorite teacher. Mrs. Hudson told the greatest stories about her adventures, and she cared about important things most adults didn't seem to care about, like secret dreams. She'd even given them an assignment about it.

September 8

Today Mrs. Hudson told us to write our secret dream on a piece of paper. I was afraid Ashley would see mine and tell, so I just scribbled on my paper. I'm writing it here in my journal instead because it is safe. MY SECRET DREAM IS TO BECOME A FAMOUS SINGER *TA-DA!* My songs will be full of emotions. People will say how I used to be so quiet, they had no idea who I really was. Ashley Chaffin will get asked for her autograph, but only because she grew up with me. I LOVE THAT PART!!!

———————————

Now Becky looked over at Ashley, who was whispering to Channa, and she was glad all over again that she hadn't risked having Ashley find out her secret dream.

Mrs. Hudson gave the two pots one final stir each. "Done to perfection," she said. "Line up for food, please. And don't forget to say *asante.*"

Everyone except Becky scrambled up quickly, the boys pushing to be first in line. Mrs. Hudson shot them a look of disapproval and they stopped dead in their tracks. Becky got up and slowly joined the line.

Sara Bowder, short and cute, with red hair and freckles she hated, inhaled deeply. "Yum, it smells so good, doesn't it?" she asked Becky.

"Yuck," Ashley said, making a face. "You're not actually going to eat that gunk, are you, Sara?"

Sara's face reddened. "Well, I—"

"I wouldn't feed that to our dog," Ashley said.

"Me either," Sara agreed quickly. "I was joking."

Becky looked away. Before middle school, Sara had been her best friend. They had done everything together. But now Sara did whatever Ashley told her to do, and she was friends with Becky only when Ashley decided it was okay.

The line moved up. Ashley shook her beaded braids off her face. "So, I've been thinking about the talent contest auditions tomorrow," she went on to Sara, completely ignoring Becky. "Who do you think my competition is?"

Sara half turned to Becky. "Are you auditioning?"

The end-of-the-school-year, sixth-grade talent contest was a Briarly tradition. The winner got a blue ribbon, and his or her photo was placed in the glass display case outside the principal's office. It was a very big deal.

More than anything, Becky longed to win the contest. She'd been practicing her favorite song, "The Lion Sleeps Tonight," every night, pretending that her hairbrush was a microphone. The problem was, she was afraid she wouldn't have the nerve to actually sing it in front of anyone, which made the possibility of her secret dream's ever coming true kind of remote. Singing in chorus was one thing. Singing a solo was something else entirely.

Mrs. Hudson had posted inspirational Swahili sayings from Tanzania all over her classroom, like USISAFIRIE NYOTA YA MWENZIO: DON'T SET SAIL USING SOMEONE ELSE'S STAR and USIPOKIFATA, HUTAKIPATA: IF YOU DON'T REACH, YOU'RE NEVER GOING TO GRAB WHAT YOU'RE AFTER. But what Becky wanted was a saying about how to get brave enough to reach for your star in the first place.

"Uh, Earth to Becky?" Ashley called. "Didn't you hear me? I just asked you something."

"I'm sorry," Becky said quickly.

Ashley rolled her eyes. "I said you're too much of a little mouseburger to audition for the talent contest."

Becky felt as if she couldn't breathe. "I might."

"But you'd have to sing *solo,*" Ashley said, as if she could smell Becky's exact fear.

Becky's cheeks burned. "I probably won't get in," she managed to say, "but I could audition."

Sara risked smiling at her. "You'll get in, Becky."

Ashley gave Sara a vicious look.

"Well, she might get in," Sara amended meekly.

Ashley inspected her perfect nails. "I once knew this girl who was so nervous about singing in front of people that she broke out in hives and her eyes puffed up and her throat swelled shut until she choked to death."

Becky could feel her hands grow clammy and her throat swell, even as Ashley spoke.

The line moved forward. Mrs. Hudson spooned a mound each of *ugali* and stew into each student's hand-carved wooden bowl. Sara got her bowl filled. She said, *"Asante,"* "Thank you" in Swahili. Then Becky. *"Asante."* Then Ashley.

"Asante. Mmmm, smells dee-lish, Mrs. Hudson!" Ashley chirped. As they turned back toward the bleachers, she stuck a finger into her mouth and pretended to gag.

The heavy aroma of the stew made Becky's head swim.

Sara peered at her. "Are you okay?"

"Fine." Becky barely moved her lips.

Ashley edged next to Sara. "When Hudson isn't looking, let's dump this—oh, great, she's looking right at us." With a fake smile on her face, Ashley waved to the teacher. "Take a big bite, you two, so she'll think we're all eating this junk."

Sara complied eagerly.

"Take a bite, Becky," Ashley ordered.

"I'm sorry, I'm not really hungry."

"Do it anyway." Ashley put her hand under Becky's bowl and pushed it upward so that the *ugali* and stew were practically in Becky's face. Becky began to gag. She sucked in air, but she couldn't seem to suck it in fast enough.

"Becky? Are you okay? Becky?"

Sara sounded very far away. Becky opened her mouth to answer her, but instead she fell to the grass, the bright Indian summer sun shining on her beaded hair, the hot *ugali* and stew splattering across her beautiful *kanga*.

And then there was nothing at all.

CHAPTER TWO

The Competition

THE SUN was barely peeking up over the horizon as Shlep scrambled up the mahogany tree. He felt sure there wasn't enough light for any of the zebras to see him, but just in case, he popped the squirming millipede into his mouth as quickly as he could. Delicious.

Instantly he felt ashamed. Real zebras didn't eat insects. He knew he should live on grass and dirty pond water, just like the rest of the herd. But too often when a savory bug crawled by, one of his paws would scoop up the treat as if the paw had a mind of its own.

It wasn't entirely his fault, he decided. He was stressed. Stress always made him hungry. Who wouldn't

be stressed, knowing that the Mara River was out there?

It was early autumn now, the rainy season long over. Ice Z was leading the herd steadily north in search of food and water. Tens of thousands of other zebra herds were doing the same thing. A long and sometimes terrifying journey lay before them, predators stalking them all the way.

But Shlep feared the Mara River more than he feared all the predators put together. The Mara was like some terrible nightmare—hundreds of thousands of wildebeests and zebras desperately braving its dangerous currents in an effort to reach the plentiful grass on the other side. Some always drowned. During the last Mara crossing, two foals and a mare from Ice Z's herd had been swept downstream into the snapping jaws of the waiting crocodiles.

Shlep had badly wanted to swim across the Mara that day, like all the other zebras. But as soon as he'd set one toe in the water, he had such an anxiety attack that he made monkey screeches and tore out tufts of his own fur. Finally, just as he had every time the herd crossed the Mara, he had jumped onto Ice Z's back, shut his eyes, and hung on for dear life.

It was so humiliating.

He sighed. He was an appalling zebra. He couldn't

quit eating bugs. Instead of running with the zebras when predators attacked, he always scrambled up the nearest tree. And he was too petrified to swim across the Mara.

No wonder Ice Z and Papa Zeke hadn't asked him to join the herd. He didn't deserve it.

But then it hit him. He could change. It wasn't impossible. Shlep swung down to the ground, full of excitement. He just had to tell someone.

"Hey, hey, Zuzi! Zip! Zap!" he shouted. "Guess what, you guys? Next time we cross the Mara, I'm gonna be brave and . . ."

His voice petered out, because no zebra was listening.

AT THAT MOMENT, the herd itself was far too excited to bother with Shlep. The night before, Papa Zeke had made a momentous announcement: When the worst threat from predators ebbed with first light, there would be a competition. Each zebra would demonstrate his or her greatest skill or talent, the winner to receive the most amazing prize in the history of amazing prizes. No zebra could imagine what it might be, but all felt certain it was something truly wonderful.

"All right, my zebra children," Papa Zeke called, "time to begin. Everyone should have signed up by marking the dirt near the mahogany tree. Who is first?"

"Begin with the best, why look at the rest?" Zilch called out as he headed for an old termite mound that would serve as the zebras' stage.

"Zilch is the best, Zilch is the best!" little Zero chanted. The young colt had miraculously escaped death earlier in the year, when the marauding lions had suddenly changed course to attack two hyenas instead of him.

"Thank you for that unsolicited testimonial," Zilch said, bowing dramatically. The others mumbled and rolled their eyes, save for Ice Z, Zip, and Zap, who were on watch.

Zilch turned his head slightly (he'd studied his reflection in pond water and knew his right profile was superior to his left) and began to recite dramatically:

"A marvelous discourse by marvelous *moi*, Zilch the zebra. I, Zilch, handsome and fearless stallion, am a Burchell's plains-dwelling zebra, vastly superior to the ugly and puny Cape mountain zebras. Though a bachelor—by choice, I might add—I risk my life and well-muscled limbs to protect and defend my herd."

"We're not your herd, we're Ice Z's herd," one of the younger fillies interrupted.

"I'll thank you to butt out of my *solo* recitation,"

Zilch snapped. "And might I add that I am my own zebra."

The herd quarreled over this until Papa Zeke *kwa*'d for quiet. "Thank you, Zilch, that was very . . . dramatic."

"But there's more," Zilch protested.

"Zilch, sometimes less *is* more," Papa Zeke said. "Who's next?"

Zilch trotted off to loud jeers as Zuzi climbed the mound, batted her eyelashes, and began to sing and dance. Unfortunately she was not very graceful, nor could she carry a tune, though she did have lovely, long eyelashes.

"Thank you, Zuzi." Papa Zeke cut her off when he couldn't take any more. "Wonderful effort."

One by one, each zebra performed, until only Xerxes and the zebras on watch were left. Xerxes said he didn't care about auditioning; he and two other stallions stood guard as Ice Z, Zip, and Zap climbed the termite mound.

Ice Z cut an impressive figure. At four feet, seven inches, and nearly seven hundred pounds, he was the biggest zebra in the herd. The stripes on his muscular body were widely spaced, but they narrowed so much near his eyes that he looked as if he were wearing sunglasses. His mane was shorter and stiffer than the

other stallions' and stood straight up in a rakish fashion.

"Mares and stallions, fillies, colts, and foals," Ice Z
began. "My two main mares and I have formed a little
trio for this occasion. We call ourselves—"

"The Z'bras!" Zip and Zap said together.

Ice Z bobbed his head in agreement. "This is a tune
we wrote on watch last night. We call it—"

"Z-Z-Z-Z Zebras, of Course," Zip and Zap said.

Ice Z gave them a cue and they began to sing, Ice Z
on lead, the mares on harmony.

Wee-oo, baboon-a rhino-rhino
Wee-oo, baboon-a rhino-rhino
Way out in Africa on the savanna,
When it comes to being cool we're top banana.
We're pretty and we're toothy, with kissable lips.
We know what's happening, we're naturally hip.
We got a hoofy, hoofy strut that says we're bad.
Cruisin' all the water holes, that's our bag.
We ain't a lion, a monkey, or a candy-striped horse
We're the zuh, zuh, zuh, zuh
Z-Z-Z-Z-Z-Z zebras, of course!
Wee-oo, baboon-a rhino-rhino
Wee-oo, baboon-a rhino-rhino
We ain't a lion, a monkey, or a candy-striped horse

We're the zuh, zuh, zuh, zuh
Z-Z-Z-Z-Z-Z zebras, of course!

By the last chorus, most of the herd was singing and prancing to the infectious beat. When the song ended, they stomped their hooves and *kwa*'d with gusto. Up in his tree, Shlep jumped around and sang, " 'Wee-oo, baboon-a rhino-rhino!' " long after the others had stopped.

"Congratulations, Z'bras," Papa Zeke cried over the din. "You're the winners!"

Ice Z, Zip, and Zap butted heads with happiness as the herd cheered. That was when Shlep realized that something wasn't right. He jumped down from the tree and hurried over to Papa Zeke, pulling on the old zebra's foreleg repeatedly to get his attention.

"Yes, Shlepper, what is it?"

"The contest can't be over. I didn't audition yet."

"*You?*" Zilch asked. "How droll."

"How silly," Zuzi added.

"You're too short," Zero said with a laugh.

"You're too green," Xerxes added.

"You're a monkey," the entire herd said, as they'd said at least five thousand times before.

"No, I'm a zebra. One of you guys. Part of the herd."

Nearly all the herd snorted with disdain.

"Oh, yeah, well, soon I'll prove what a great zebra I am," Shlep mumbled.

"Climb onto my back, Shlepper," Papa Zeke offered kindly, "while I tell the Z'bras what they won."

Shlep scrambled onto Papa Zeke's back. The old zebra grunted. "You must be eating a lot of beetles, Shlepper."

"Nah, zebras don't eat insects," Shlep ventured.

"I see," Papa Zeke said, nodding. He turned back to the herd. "So, my zebra children, time to announce what the Z'bras have won. They have won a trip to . . ." He indulged in a dramatic pause. ". . . to the human world!"

Every zebra *kwa*'d at once. This was a shocking development. The zebras knew there were humans, of course. Ever since safari tour buses had begun to bring humans to the Serengeti, even the shyest zebra had learned about them. Unarmed humans were harmless, rather funny-looking, and had some very strange habits.

What's more, like all zebras, those in Ice Z's herd had extremely sensitive ears, which easily overheard human conversations, taped music, and radio broadcasts on the buses. Some zebras had even developed a taste for opera or rock music. And listening to silly advertisements for items no zebra could ever use was a favorite herd entertainment.

But only Papa Zeke had actually gone to the human world. And that, he said, had been a long, long time ago.

When the zebras finally settled down, Papa Zeke spoke again. "There is more to tell. You've all seen and heard the humans. But what you do not know is this: Our herd has its very own human. It is to our human, far, far away, that the Z'bras will travel."

Chaos erupted anew as the herd argued about whether or not this could possibly be true.

"Point of order! Point of order!" Zilch bellowed, rearing up on his hind legs to get everyone's attention. "Papa Zeke, only you have been to the human world. Why breach protocol now? And why send *them*?" He lifted his snout contemptuously at the Z'bras.

Papa Zeke shrugged, almost unseating Shlep. "Traveling to a world that is not your own takes youth and energy. I am an old zebra, nearing the end of my days."

"Don't say that, Papa Zeke," Zuzi said. She nuzzled her nose against his.

"Not saying it won't make it not true. One more trip to the human world would most likely kill me. It's time to teach others to carry on. This is the way of our world."

"We're honored that you chose us . . . ," Ice Z said. Zip and Zap nodded their agreement.

". . . But we can't go," Ice Z added. "That is, *I* can't go. I have responsibilities. Who will watch over the herd?"

"Some of us are quite capable of watching over ourselves, thank you." Zilch sniffed.

"Brother Ice," Xerxes called out, "I'll watch over the herd."

Ice Z flared his nostrils and walked over to him. Their eyes locked.

"Only until you come back, of course," Xerxes added.

"Good," Ice Z told Xerxes, his voice steely. "Because I *will* come back. And when I do come back, I expect to find my herd just like I left my herd."

"Uh, that would include me, right, Ice Z?" Shlep asked.

"Just like I left my herd," Ice Z repeated.

"Exactly," Papa Zeke agreed. "So it's all settled."

Zip and Zap nodded. "But what are we supposed to do once we get there?"

The old zebra twitched his huge ears. "This is a very good question. And the answer to your very good question is . . . I don't know. The only one who would know exactly is Zink the zebra. Zink the zebra, the—"

"—wisest zebra of all," the herd chorused, since they had heard Papa Zeke tell this story so many times, "with the most courage and the biggest heart."

"Exactly," Papa Zeke agreed. "Zink would know."

"Isn't Zink just a made-up story?" Zuzi asked.

Papa Zeke shrugged. "My beloved great-grand-mother of blessed memory—"

"May she rest in peace," the herd intoned.

"—said she had a friend from another herd, Zaidey zebra, who had a sister who had a cousin by marriage, Zechariah zebra, who claimed he once drank dirty pond water next to a splendiferous polka-dotted zebra named Zink."

The zebras oohed. They hadn't heard this part before.

"But," Papa Zeke went on, "I heard this Zechariah zebra was a big liar. So the answer to your question is . . ."

He bent down to bite off some tough grass with his sharp front teeth and swallowed slowly while the herd held its collective breath.

"The answer to your question is . . . I don't know."

The herd groaned.

"I do not, however, send you to the human world unprepared, Z'bras," Papa Zeke added dramatically.

He touched his nose softly against Zip's, then Zap's,

and finally against Ice Z's nose. Each felt a strange and wonderful electricity inside his or her head.

"There," Papa Zeke said. "Now you have The Power."

"Wow!" Zap breathed in an awe-filled voice.

Zip turned to Zap. "Do you have any idea what Papa Zeke is talking about?"

"No," Zap admitted sheepishly. "But it sounds exciting, doesn't it?"

"Wisdom does not come overnight," Papa Zeke intoned. "And now, Z'bras, you must go."

Ice Z eyed Xerxes again. The scarred zebra flashed him a mirthless smile that made Shlep shiver and made Ice Z very uneasy. "What's the hurry?" Ice Z asked Papa Zeke.

Papa Zeke's voice turned grave as his dark eyes took in the sweep of the savanna. "Our human is in terrible danger. There is a predator stalking very close."

"What melodrama!" Zilch sniffed. "I don't believe we even have a human."

"Ignorance is not always bliss, Zilch," Papa Zeke said. "Sometimes it is just ignorance." He headed slowly for the mahogany tree. "And now I am a very tired old zebra. Shlep and I will be in the shade, napping."

"Wait, Papa Zeke!" Ice Z called. "Who's our human?"

Papa Zeke turned around. "I forgot to say?"

The entire herd nodded.

He shook his head sadly. "They say the mind is the first thing to go. All right, then, my zebra children. Here it is. Our human's name is Becky Zaslow."

CHAPTER THREE

The Needle

WHEN BECKY WOKE UP, she had no idea where she was. The room was dark, its shadows sinister. Her arm hurt. Something was stuck in it. She was alone. No, wait. There was her mom, asleep on a chair near the window. But why would her mom be—

It all rushed back to her at once, every terrible moment slamming into her consciousness.

She'd fainted in front of the entire sixth grade.

When she'd come to, Mrs. Hudson had been cradling her head while the school nurse, Ms. Bingham, took her pulse from her wrist. The principal and some other teachers had pushed back a ring of gawking kids.

Ms. Bingham had noticed the bruises on Becky's legs and lifted the bottom of Becky's *kanga* for a better look. Brian Green had snickered loudly, and some of the boys had laughed. Becky couldn't believe the nurse had lifted her dress like that, with all those boys staring down at her.

She'd been put on a stretcher and into the back of an ambulance, as if she'd been in a really bad car accident. Mrs. Hudson rode with her. Becky had been wheeled into the emergency room, where a doctor looked into her eyes with a light, examined her bruises, and felt the sides of her neck.

It had hurt when he pressed down. Becky didn't say a word.

Then a stern-faced nurse had told Becky her mother was on her way and that she should change into a paper gown so a different doctor could see her. Mrs. Hudson had helped her into the gown; it was embarrassing because the gown had no back.

As Becky changed, an idea of what was wrong had flown into her mind. It made her vibrate with fear. But she didn't say a word.

Mrs. Hudson had stayed until Mrs. Zaslow arrived. Becky's mom had held her hand all afternoon as a doctor with a big stomach supervised other doctors who examined every part of her, including private parts even her mom didn't see anymore. Nurses stuck needles in her arm to take blood. It hurt. Everything hurt. But Becky never said so.

All she'd said was, "I'm fine."

All her mother had said was, "I'm sure it's just the flu." But her eyes said something different.

Becky's tall, handsome father walked in, still in his policeman's uniform, and gently hugged her. He brought all the right things: her flannel pajamas, jelly doughnuts, the raggedy stuffed zebra she'd slept with ever since he'd given it to her on her sixth birthday, and her secret journal.

But the stern-faced nurse put Becky's journal on a chair with her stew-splattered *kanga* and wouldn't let Becky change into her pajamas because Becky was still in the emergency room. And after she noticed that the doughnut smell made Becky nauseous, she took the doughnuts to the nurses' station.

Her mom put a cool cloth on her forehead, and her parents assured her over and over that she just had the flu.

Becky thought, *If I don't say anything, I can't say the wrong thing.* And: *If I don't write it in my journal, it won't be true.* So she clutched her stuffed zebra, kept her mouth shut, and didn't ask for her journal back, even though she'd already figured out what was wrong with her.

It had nothing to do with the flu.

Finally the doctor with the big stomach came back. He had a fake smile on his face and his voice was too loud and hearty. He wanted Becky to stay overnight so they could do one more test in the morning, and he wanted to take her parents for a walk down the hall, so they could talk.

That's when she knew for *sure* what was wrong with her.

She had AIDS.

THE ORDERLY'S NAME was Shaquille. His gym shoes had purple lightning bolts on them. He said he'd be taking Becky for a little ride. Her mom helped her onto the gurney and Shaquille rolled her into an elevator and down to the third floor while her mom trotted alongside. She told Becky about some new books in the bookstore, where she was assistant manager. Her words popped in Becky's mind like bubbles from a soapy wand; there, then gone.

The sign on the wall said PEDIATRIC ONCOLOGY. Becky knew the word *pediatric* but had no idea what *oncology* meant. People in white jackets scurried around, looking important. A child somewhere cried, "No more needles!" over and over. A man hurried by with a bunch of aluminum-colored balloons that all read GET WELL SOON. Her mom went on and on about books—*pop! pop! pop!*—as if she was afraid to be quiet.

Shaquille wheeled Becky into an examination room, told her to stay sweet, and took off again on his lightning bolts. A slender young woman with short blond hair bustled in.

"Good morning, Becky, I'm Patsi Goddall—call me Pat," she said briskly. "I'm the nurse-practitioner who works with Dr. Franklin. He'll be here shortly to do your bone marrow aspiration. Do you have any questions about it?"

"I've already explained it to her," Becky's mother said quickly. "She knows it's like taking blood, only from inside her hipbone. And it might hurt a little."

Pat's eyebrows shot up. Becky's eyes slid to her mom.

"It'll be fine, Becks." Her mom squeezed her hand.

Dr. Franklin, the one with the big stomach, came into the room and began to scrub his hands at the washbasin. He had perfect hair, like the actors who played doctors on TV.

An intern and a technician moved Becky to a table covered with white paper and placed her on her stomach, a pillow under her right hip.

"You okay, Becky?" Pat asked.

No-no-no-no, her mind cried.

"Fine," she said. She shut her eyes, but not before she saw Dr. Franklin lift up a syringe. The needle was so huge it looked like one from a cartoon. But it was real.

"I know this is scary, Becky," Pat said as she helped Dr. Franklin prepare. "You okay?"

"Fine." In her head, she sang an African spiritual Mrs. Hudson had taught them.

> *Went to the rock to hide my face;*
> *Rock cried out "No hiding place!"*

Pat pulled Becky's panties down without even asking.

> *Went to the well to drown my pain;*
> *Well cried out "I see your shame!"*

"I'll tell you everything before Dr. Franklin does it," Pat promised. "No surprises."

Her mother's hand tightened around hers. "I'm right here, sweetie," she told her daughter. "I'm right here."

Becky clenched her eyes shut even harder. Pat described everything: the swab of antiseptic to prevent germs, the stinging shot of anesthetic like the novocaine she got at the dentist before she had a cavity filled.

"Okay, here comes the tough part, Becky," Pat continued. "Dr. Franklin is going to push the needle into your bone to get a marrow sample. Stay absolutely still."

What were the rest of the words to that spiritual? Becky couldn't remember. But she had to remember, she had to, or this would be real and—

Someone else was singing now, very softly, Becky's favorite song. Her mother, her lips at Becky's ear.

In the jungle, the mighty jungle, the lion sleeps tonight.
In the jungle, the mighty jungle, the lion sleeps
    tonight. . . .

The pain was burning-coal red; it spread through her until there was nothing in the world but pain. Becky couldn't hear her mom singing because someone was moaning too loudly.

The someone was her.

"All done," Dr. Franklin said.

Becky opened her eyes. The technician was holding a syringe full of bright red liquid that had come from inside her bone. Pat put a dressing on her hip, and Dr. Franklin told her to lie there and rest.

CHAPTER FOUR

The Diagnosis

September 29

It is easier to write the truth when it is GOOD NEWS!!!
I don't have AIDS!!! Doctor Franklin told us that I have
leukemia. It is a kind of cancer inside my bone marrow,
where blood is formed. He said everyone's blood has white
and red cells. The white cells fight off infections. But
when you get leukemia, the white cells are too immature
(like my little brother, Lee, I said, ha-ha) to fight off infections, which is why I have felt so sick. An immature white
cell is called a blast (something I am <u>not</u> having, ha-ha).
When you get leukemia, you get a lot of blasts.

After Dr. Franklin left, Mom said I have to stay in the
hospital while I have a medicine called chemotherapy. She

said it might make me feel sick for a little while, and my hair might get thinner (boo!), but it won't hurt like the bone marrow test did, and afterwards I'll be fine (yeah!). She promised to bring me all of my homework every day so I don't get behind in school.

Mom was surprised that I was not upset. I told her I thought I was dying from AIDS, so even though leukemia is bad, it is not <u>that</u> bad. That made both of us laugh!!! I have been getting antibiotics through a needle in my arm that already makes me feel better. When Dad gets here I will beg him to talk Mom into letting me go to the talent contest auditions tonight. After what happened yesterday, if I don't go, everyone will think I really <u>do</u> have AIDS.

Mom will be tough but Dad will be on my side. When he really wants her to do something, he kisses the back of her neck, which she always says she can't resist. He may have to kiss her neck <u>a lot</u> to get her to give in. Wish me luck!!!

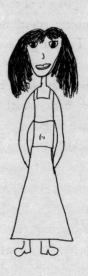

CHAPTER FIVE

The Roommate

September 29 (still)

I can't believe how happy I was just a few hours ago.
Everything is horrible. Dad asked Mom about the
auditions and kissed the back of her neck, but instead of
giving in, she got mad. She said my immune system is
bad from leukemia so I can't fight off germs and school
is full of germs that could make me sick. Well, I already
<u>am</u> sick, so I don't see what difference it could make!!!
Then Dad said that since I could not do anything fun
for a long time maybe I could go to the audition tonight
and start chemotherapy tomorrow. They had a big, horrible fight. It was all my fault and it was even worse than
having cancer. I said I was sorry but they were too busy

fighting to hear me. They just left to go to the billing office and—

———————————

The door opened. Becky looked up from her journal as Pat stuck her head into the room.

"Becky, you're about to get a roommate."

Becky shoved her journal under her pillow. "I am?"

Before Pat could say anything else, a tall, very thin girl sailed into the room. It was impossible to tell how old she was. She had beautiful long blond hair and wore a lot of makeup. She was so skinny that Becky could see the outline of her ribs beneath her stretchy top. Her skirt was the size of a postage stamp, her shoes high-heeled.

"Ah, home sweet home," the girl said with a sneer. She dumped a graffiti-covered backpack on the other bed, plopped down, and looked coolly over at Becky. "And who might you be?"

"Darlene, Becky Zaslow," Pat answered. "Becky, Darlene Dunbar. You guys both have cancer, and you'll both be getting chemo."

"Thrilling." Darlene yawned ostentatiously. "*Maman* and *Papa* are with the number crunchers," she added. She said *"Maman"* and *"Papa,"* with the emphasis on the last syllable, as if she were French.

"Ah, *oui*," Pat said dryly. "Becky, I'll be back soon to start your chemo IV. And Darlene, try to be nice. I know it's a stretch."

Pat shut the door behind her as Darlene pulled a cosmetics case out of her backpack and added even more blush to her bright pink cheeks. Finally she turned to Becky, striking a dramatic pose.

"Well?" she asked.

Becky had no idea what she wanted.

"My *makeup*. What do you *think*?" Darlene demanded. "Be brutal."

Becky gulped. "It's . . . kind of a lot."

"What do you know?" Darlene snorted, shaking her golden hair off her face. "I happen to look very sophisticated."

"I'm sorry." Becky reached for her raggedy zebra.

Darlene gave Becky and the zebra a long, disdainful once-over. "How old are you, *six*?"

"Ten and a half."

"Figures. I'm twelve." Darlene took a compact out of her backpack and surveyed herself in the mirror. "So what kind of cancer do you have, dear?"

"Leukemia."

"The good kind or the bad kind?" Darlene rummaged through her backpack, pulling out jewelry.

Becky squeezed her zebra. "What's the good kind?"

"A-L-L, of course. Everyone knows that."

Becky looked at her blankly.

"Acute lymphoblastic leukemia? Ring any bells?"

Becky shook her head.

"How about A-M-L, then? Acute myelogenous leukemia?"

"My mom just said leukemia."

"Serious rookie," Darlene muttered as she slid a rhinestone bracelet onto her bony arm. "You'd better ask. If you have ALL, you'll probably live. If you have AML, you'll probably die."

"My mom said I'll get better. It must be the good kind." Becky tried to keep her voice from shaking.

"Not necessarily," Darlene said, twisting the bracelet around and admiring it. "Some parents are so juvenile about these things. For example, I have Hodgkin's disease. I suppose you don't know what that is, either."

Becky shook her head again.

"Cancer of the lymph nodes, which produce white blood cells to fight infections," Darlene recited in a bored singsong. "When I first got Hodgkin's, I was stage two. That means I had it in two places on the same side. So I got radiation and chemo and went into remission."

"You got better?" Becky asked.

"Then I got worse again. That's relapsing. This is my second relapse in a year, which is very bad."

"I'm sorry," Becky said.

"Please, it's not like I'm going to *die* or anything," Darlene scoffed. "My parents think I will, though. But when they're with me they *pretend* they think I'm going to get better. That's what I mean about being juvenile."

"They lie to you, you mean," Becky said.

Darlene nodded. "And they feel so-o-o guilty, even though it's not their fault. Which is why I can get them to do whatever I want. Like buy me this outfit. And this jewelry. And all this makeup." She dropped her head back against her pillows like an actress playing a death scene. "And *that* is the end of my tragic little tale."

Becky nodded too. She didn't want to say the wrong thing.

"Tonight," Darlene went on, "I'll tell them to get me a big-screen TV, a new VCR, and every single video I want."

"Would they really get you all that?"

"Of course." Darlene got up and wobbled in her high heels over to the window that looked out onto the lawn and the parking lot.

"Or maybe I'll tell them to buy me my own car," Darlene decided. "A red convertible."

"But . . . you're not old enough to drive."

Darlene turned to her. "So? I'll just sit in it. And when I'm sixteen, I'll make them buy me a new one. All I have to do is guilt-jerk 'em."

"What does that mean?"

Darlene tossed her hair back. "Didn't anyone tell you the side effects when you get chemo, dear?"

"My mom did. A little."

"Well, first you show them your inner beauty, meaning you barf your guts out. Parents can't stand to see that."

Becky felt nauseous just hearing about it.

"And then"—Darlene grinned—"there's the best guilt-jerk of all." She wobbled over to Becky's bed and sat next to her. "Know what that is?"

"No."

Darlene put her hands on top of her own head, grabbed two fistfuls of her beautiful blond hair, and yanked. It all came off in her hands. Under the wig, she was totally bald.

"Ta-da!" she cried, leering into Becky's face. "All your hair falls out!"

Darlene jumped up and danced around the room, a painted, prancing skeleton. With a witchlike cackle, she swung back to Becky, who cowered in mute horror.

When Darlene saw that, her face changed. "Wait. You really didn't know? *Really* really?"

Becky dug her nails into her zebra. "No."

"Your mom *lied* to you, then," Darlene said. She twirled her wig on one finger. "I *hate* liars. I *always* tell the truth. Do you?"

"I try to," Becky said softly.

"Okay, then, tell me the truth," Darlene said. "Do I look ugly?"

Becky's mouth opened. Nothing came out.

"It's a simple question. Do. I. Look. Ugly?"

"Yes," Becky finally said. "I'm sorry," she added quickly.

"Well, at least you told *half* the truth, which makes you only *half* as bad as the other liars." Darlene headed for the door, then turned back to Becky. "I do look ugly. But the truth is, you aren't really sorry at all."

CHAPTER SIX

The Crossing

ICE Z TURNED to Zip and Zap. "Ready?"

The mares nodded solemnly.

When Papa Zeke had told the Z'bras they'd be going to the human world, they'd had no idea what to do. But now, with The Power, they seemed to *know* things, as if the old zebra were inside their minds, guiding them.

For example, though Papa Zeke was now asleep, he had just explained exactly how to make the crossing.

Gallop together in perfect stride, Z'bras, his silent voice inside their minds had said. *Turn your feelings, imagination, and spirit to the story of Zink the zebra, then leap for the sun. If you believe the story with all your heart, you will cross over to the human world.*

The moment had come. Ice Z gave Xerxes one last look of warning. Then he *kwa*'d softly, and the Z'bras began to walk toward the other zebras, then trot, as one.

"Good luck, you guys!" Shlep called to them.

In silent awe, the herd parted as the Z'bras picked up their pace to a canter, then to a gallop. Their hooves thundered, their powerful bodies were obscured by flying dust.

"Kwa!" Ice Z barked a command.

The three zebras leaped for the sun. With all their feelings, imagination, and spirit, they filled their hearts with the story of Zink. And they believed.

The sky above the Serengeti flashed from blue to purple to the brightest pink as gorgeous music filled the air. Then the Z'bras were no longer in Africa, or any place that had a name. In the space between the beats of their hearts, they whooshed into a tunnel of light and landed in another world, far, far away.

They were jammed together, head to rump to head, in a large closet with a narrow door. The walls were floor-to-ceiling shelving, filled with towels, blankets, and sheets.

You are in a hospital supply closet, they heard Papa Zeke say in their minds.

"Where's Becky?" Zap wondered aloud.

In the room next door, to the right.

"We have a slight problem," Ice Z said. "It's called size. We can't move."

If you need to be small, think "small." You'll shrink to the size and shape of a Cape mountain zebra foal.

"Now, that is above and beyond the call of duty," Zip said, her nostrils quivering with indignation. "A *Cape mountain* zebra? We don't even speak to other *Burchell's* zebras if they're not in our herd!"

Zap nodded. "Besides, we're black with white stripes. They're white with black stripes."

"Definitely not *our* kind of zebra," the mares said.

That is a very bad attitude. Besides, it's temporary. When you want to grow again, think "big."

"Oh"—Zap gave a toothy grin—"that's a warthog of a different color."

"Ready to try it, friends, *rafikis*?" Ice Z asked.

Small, they thought.

They shrank; their heads became plumper, their ears grew longer, and their stripes rearranged themselves. Now they were no more than thirty inches high.

"You're very funny-looking." Zap giggled at Zip.

"Now what?" Ice Z sighed.

There is a time for everything. You wait.

* * *

As soon as Pat walked through the door, Becky asked if it was true.

"Is what true?" Pat carried a tray of supplies, including a plastic bag of chemotherapy medicine. She hung the chemo bag atop Becky's IV pole.

"That I'll lose all my hair like Darlene did?"

"I thought your parents talked with you." Pat set up Becky's IV line.

"They did. My mom said my hair might get thinner from the chemotherapy. But she didn't say I'd be *bald*!"

Pat stopped and took in Becky's pale, anxious face. "Not everyone goes bald from chemo, Becky," she said gently.

"But it's possible," Becky said.

"Yes, it's possible," Pat agreed. "The medicines we give you to fight the leukemia are very strong. But they have to be strong, because leukemia is a tough enemy."

"Like a predator." Becky squeezed her toy zebra.

"Right. So while the chemo is fighting the bad guys— the predators—it's pretty tough on the good guys, too. That's why you can feel sick or lose your hair. But it's temporary. After a while you'll feel better. And if you do lose your hair, it will grow back."

Becky's hair was still braided from Africa Day. She pressed the braids to her head as if she could will her hair not to fall out. "I'll look so ugly," she said. "No one will want to be my friend."

Pat had seen this reaction from kids many times before. She took Becky's hand. "You really need to talk some more with your parents. But I have to start a new IV for you now, kiddo."

Slowly, having no choice, Becky held out her arm. Pat wiped the inside of Becky's elbow with an alcohol swab, then tore open a fresh needle packet.

"A stick now."

The needle pierced Becky's tender flesh, and she clenched her teeth.

"Hurts, huh?" Pat asked sympathetically.

Becky shook her head. "It's fine."

"It's okay to tell the truth, Becky."

Pat double-checked the line leading to the chemo to make sure the medicine was flowing properly. "It can help if you talk about things—what hurts, what scares you, or—"

Pat stopped midsentence. Clearly, Becky wasn't listening. Instead she was staring out the open door of her room, almost as if she were somewhere else completely. Pat had seen that before too. So she picked up the now-empty tray and quietly left the room.

CHAPTER SEVEN

The Meeting

IT'S TIME, *my zebra children.*

The Z'bras, who had been waiting for what felt like forever in the supply closet, scrambled to their feet. Ice Z carefully pushed the closet door open with one hoof and peeked into the hallway. Humans were everywhere, and they all seemed to be in a hurry.

Go now. Only our human will see and hear you.

Despite Papa Zeke's assurance, the Z'bras edged into the hall and hugged their bodies to the wall, inching along until they reached Becky's room. Her door was open. They stuck their heads in, one atop the other.

A small, thin, pale girl was in a bed, medicine flow-

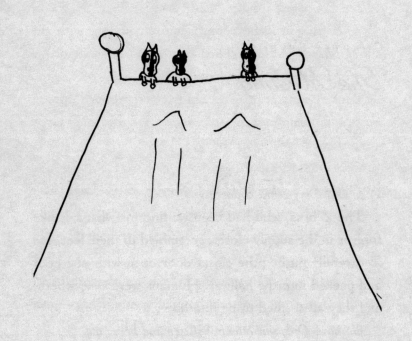

ing through a plastic line into her arm. She clutched a raggedy stuffed zebra. A blond nurse stood nearby.

The Z'bras ducked back into the hall.

"Becky," Ice Z whispered with surprise. "Why, she's just a little girl, a *msichana*!"

"Our *msichana*," Zap said. "I love her already."

Ice Z nodded tersely. "Let's do it."

They slid into the room, almost colliding with the nurse on her way out. Then they stood in a line at the foot of Becky's bed. And smiled.

Becky's eyes grew wide and her jaw dropped open.

"Close your mouth, silly," Zap laughed. "Do you want a sweat bee to fly in?"

Becky didn't move.

"Hmmm," Zip mused. "Maybe they don't have sweat bees here. Lucky dik-diks."

"Humans say lucky *ducks*," Zap corrected proudly. "I heard it on the radi—"

"*Rafikis,*" Ice Z interrupted, "can we please focus?"

The mares nodded, and then, giving Becky their toothiest grins, all three zebras said, "Hi!"

"I'm Zip."

"I'm Zap."

"And I'm Ice Z," the stallion added with a dapper shake of his mane.

"We're the Z'bras!"

"I'm dreaming, right?" Becky asked slowly.

The Z'bras shook their heads in unison.

"But I have to be dreaming. I'm talking to three teeny little zebras. Zebras can't talk."

"Wrong!" Zip and Zap hooted cheerfully.

"We also sing," Ice Z added.

"Doo-wah," they sang, in lovely three-part harmony.

Becky loves to sing. It's her favorite thing.

"Really?" Ice Z marveled. "Since you love to sing, Becky, we'll have to sing together sometime."

Sing with zebras? Becky shut her eyes, then opened them again. But the zebras were still there. "The medicine going into my arm must be making me go crazy," she said. "I never told you I sing. Besides, no one has ever seen talking—"

"—singing—" Zap added.

"—zebras."

Zap cocked her head to the side. "Well, that doesn't mean we don't exist. Have you ever seen your feelings?"

"Well, no . . . ," Becky admitted.

"Or your imagination?" Zip asked.

"No, but—"

"Or your spirit?" Ice Z put in.

Becky thought a moment. "I guess not."

Three plump zebra heads bobbed up and down. "We rest our case."

"This is just so exciting!" Zap looked around Becky's room. She spotted the window. "What's out there?"

The two mares trotted over, but as Cape mountain zebra foals, they were too short to reach it. So they sprang straight up, over and over, trying to see out.

"This could take a while," Zap said, jumping again.

"Think big," Ice Z reminded them reluctantly.

Big, they thought. Instantly the mares grew to their normal selves.

"You're gigantic!" Becky gasped. "That was incredible. Can you change your size again?"

"We're not here to play," Ice Z reminded the mares.

Zip and Zap didn't listen. *Big-small-big-small-big-small-big,* they thought, gleefully changing back and forth from tiny Cape mountain foals to huge Burchell's zebras.

"That's the most fantastic thing I ever saw," Becky told them. "You were very cute when you were little."

Zip sniffed. "We certainly didn't think so."

"Yeah," Zap agreed. "Being a funny-looking little Cape mountain zebra is no stroll in the savanna." Now that she was big again, she could see out the window.

"Wow, there's enough grass out there for ten dry seasons!" she exclaimed. "Come see, Ice Z!"

Curious in spite of himself, Ice Z loped over to the window. They looked so funny there, three huge zebras with their noses up against the glass, that Becky laughed aloud just as her mother came into the room.

"Small!" Ice Z ordered.

Instantly the Z'bras shrank to Cape mountain foal size, which made Becky laugh again.

"Becky?" her mother asked.

"Look at the zebras, Mom!"

"What zebras?" Mrs. Zaslow looked around the room; then her eyes lit on the stuffed zebra on Becky's bed. "Oh, you mean *this* zebra." She picked it up and playfully walked it across the bed.

"No, no, I mean the little zebras by the window."

"There's no one here but us, Becky."

"Wrong!" the Z'bras said cheerfully.

"They're talking. Mom, you must hear them."

"Doo-wahhh!" they sang together.

Becky laughed again. "And they sing. They're right there." She pointed at the Z'bras by the window.

Her mother looked deeply worried.

"You can't see them, Mom? Really?"

Pat stuck her head into the room. "Mrs. Zaslow, your husband called and said—"

"Something is wrong with my daughter," Mrs. Zaslow interuppted. "She's hallucinating. She says she sees little singing zebras. Get Dr. Franklin."

Pat smiled. "Don't worry about it. Kids say they see

all kinds of things during chemo. Dinosaurs, dol-
phins . . ."

"But it's very disturbing."

"I'm sorry," Becky said guiltily.

"Disturbing to you, maybe, Mrs. Zaslow," Pat said.
"Not to Becky. Look, your husband called to say he'd
meet you in the billing office in five minutes. There are
more papers to sign."

"Yes, all right." Her mother handed Becky the
stuffed zebra and touched her daughter's cheek. "I'll be
right back, Becks." Then she and Pat left.

When they were gone, Becky turned to the Z'bras.
"Why couldn't my mom see you?"

"We're your zebras, not hers," Ice Z replied.

"*My* zebras? I'm sorry, but I don't understand.
Maybe if you told me why you're here."

Why, indeed? They didn't know. How embarrassing.

But then, in a flash, they *did* know. It was as if the
knowledge had been inside their heads all along.

"It's like this," Ice Z said, walking toward her.
"We're here to take you on an adventure."

"Oh, no, I can't go anywhere," Becky said quickly.
"I have to stay here with this thing in my arm or I won't
get well."

"But it's only your body that needs the medicine,"
Zap said. "And your body isn't you, see?"

Becky frowned. "I'm sorry, but I don't see."

"It's not complicated," Ice Z assured her. "All you do is, you leave your body *here,* and come with us *there.*"

"That's impossible."

"No, it isn't," Zip told her.

"Just use your imagination," Ice Z urged. " 'If you have no imagination—' "

" '—then you have no wings,' " Becky finished, her voice awe-filled. It was one of the proverbs from East Africa that Mrs. Hudson had taped up in her classroom.

"Right," Zip agreed, her eyes flashing. "There is no failure in failure, only in not trying."

"Right!" Zap cried. "And some very good people have very bad credit!"

Ice Z and Zip looked doubtfully at Zap.

"You were giving Becky famous inspirational sayings," Zap explained. "I wanted to give her one too. That's a famous inspirational saying. Isn't it?"

"No," Zip replied. "It's a radio commercial for National Commerce Bank in Dar es Salaam."

Zap closed her eyes sheepishly. "Oh. Sorry."

Ice Z turned to Becky. "You can do it, Becky. Get out of bed. Your body will stay behind to get the medicine."

Becky looked skeptical.

"I promise," Ice Z said gently.

Slowly, tentatively, Becky lifted her left arm, the one with the IV running into it. It hurt. She dropped it back to the bed.

" 'If at first you don't succeed,' " Zip began.

" 'Try, try again,' " Becky muttered. This time she pushed her blanket back and sat up, but it made her terribly dizzy. "I can't do it. I'm sorry."

Ice Z put his front hooves on the bed and his eyes found Becky's. "It's okay to be afraid," he said softly. "Every single night when I'm on watch for predators, I'm afraid."

Becky twisted her little zebra's matted fur in her fingers but didn't say anything.

Ice Z laid his cheek against Becky's hand. "We will never lie to you. And we will never hurt you."

"We *are* you," the three Z'bras said together.

Becky had no idea what they meant. But somehow, even though it seemed crazy, she trusted them. With one hand on Ice Z's mane, she slowly got out of bed.

This time nothing hurt. And as she followed him to the door, she had the strangest sensation that her mind was expanding.

"Look," Ice Z said, cocking his head toward her bed.

She turned and looked back. There was her body, still in bed, hooked up to the IV.

"That's amazing," she said quietly.

"Think Zink," the Z'bras whispered. "Think Zink."

Zink? But before Becky could ask what Zink was, or why she should think about it, she was gone.

CHAPTER EIGHT
The Arrival

BECKY FLEW.

Lub-dub. A beat of her heart, and the sky shimmered from blue to purple and then to the brightest pink. She whooshed into a tunnel. Wonderful music filled the air. Before her heart could beat again, she landed with a bump.

Slowly she opened her eyes. She was sitting under a leafy baobab tree. There were green grass, small shrubs, and thick brush as far as the eye could see. The air was hot; there was hardly any breeze.

And she was surrounded by zebras. Big zebras.

"It's okay, Becky. It's me, Ice Z." Her eyes sought

him out in the throng of identical-looking animals. He stepped toward her, with Zip and Zap at either side. "You recognize us, right?"

"Yes, but . . ." Becky felt overwhelmed by all the stripes around her. "There are so many of you. How can I ever tell you apart?"

For some reason, the zebras found this very amusing.

A stallion with an unusually clean hide surveyed her from head to toe. "*This* is our human?" he asked disdainfully. "Pale and puny, utterly unimpressive." He trotted off, nose high in the air.

"I'm sorry," Becky called after him, then looked over at Ice Z. "I guess he doesn't like me."

"Oh, ignore him," a filly with long eyelashes advised her. "That's what we do."

Becky closed her eyes and rubbed them. But when she opened them, the herd was still there. "This is all very strange. It can't be real."

"We're as real as you are," Ice Z told her. He turned to the zebra with the long eyelashes. "Zuzi, can you introduce Becky around? We have to go on watch, and—"

"No problem, Brother Ice," a large zebra with a scar on his neck interrupted. His voice was deep, almost sinister. "I'll handle watch. Like I did while you went on *vacation.*"

Ice Z glared at him. "It wasn't *vacation* and you know it. And now that I'm back, I'll watch over *my* herd."

"Only trying to help, Brother Ice," the scarred zebra replied. Ice Z bared his teeth at him, and Becky could tell that Ice Z didn't feel very brotherly toward the scarred zebra at all. Some zebras murmured nervously, and even Becky felt uneasy.

"It's okay, Becky," Ice Z assured her.

It must really be okay, Becky decided. *Ice Z promised he'd never lie to me. And I believe him. I think.*

As the Z'bras left to go on watch, the long-eyelashed filly sat down beside Becky and daintily tucked her legs beneath her. "I'm Zuzi," she said in a girlish voice. "I love your braids."

"Thank you," Becky said shyly.

"Okay, let's see." Zuzi pointed with a foreleg. "The big scarred zebra is Xerxes. The little colt by that tree is Zero, and the big, clean, *ugly* one with him is Zilch."

"I heard that!" Zilch called. "Lions may roam and break my bones, but names can never hurt me."

"Oh, that's original." Zuzi smirked. "Anyway, Becky, welcome to the Serengeti."

"In *Africa*?" Becky gasped. "That's impossible."

"If you have no imagination," a new voice said, "then you have no wings." It was a rough and old-sounding voice, but somehow comforting. And familiar. The ring of zebras parted and an elderly zebra walked slowly toward Becky. His back was swayed, his eyelids drooped, and his hide hung slack. But Becky found him beautiful just the same. Suddenly nothing seemed strange anymore.

"So, you're here at last," the old zebra said as he stood in front of her. "Let me get a better look at you. It's been a long time."

Becky got up and brushed some grass from her pajamas. "Do you know me?"

"From forever," the old zebra said. "I am Papa Zeke—"

"—the oldest and wisest zebra in all of Africa," the zebras dutifully recited.

"Exactly," Papa Zeke agreed. "Spiritual leader of the herd. Of course, I'm really only standing in for *you*."

"For me?" Becky echoed. "What are you talking about?"

He didn't answer. Instead he paced slowly back and forth. "Tell me, how did the talent contest auditions go?"

"How do you know about that?"

"I'm very wise. So?"

"I had to have chemotherapy. I couldn't audition," Becky explained. "My parents say I'm not strong enough."

"*They* say. What do *you* say?"

Becky shrugged. "They know best. I don't mind."

Papa Zeke's ears twitched. "No?"

"No."

"So. I hear you have a bad illness. You have tests where they stick you and prick you." The old zebra flicked his tail to shoo away a sweat bee. "Does it hurt?"

"No," Becky replied. "It's for my own good."

"I see. You're very plucky, aren't you?"

"What's *plucky*?"

"Brave, noble, never complain," Papa Zeke explained.

"Oh, well, then, yes," Becky said proudly. Most of the herd was hanging on her every word, and she was starting to enjoy being the center of attention. "I try to be plucky."

"I *hate* plucky," Papa Zeke grumbled.

The other zebras gasped.

"Okay, okay, I hate *fake* plucky, you big faker, you." Papa Zeke snorted. "You think it's so brave to pretend nothing hurts, so noble to not stand up for yourself? And what's with the apologizing all the time, missy?"

"I'm sorry. Oops." Becky clapped her hand over her mouth. She had just apologized for apologizing.

Papa Zeke walked toward her until her back touched the tree. His rheumy eyes scowled into hers. *But I'm not afraid of him,* Becky realized with surprise. *And I know I can tell him the truth. Just like I can write the truth in my journal. I don't know how I know, but I just do.*

She took a deep breath. "I *did* mind not auditioning for the talent show," she admitted, her voice small.

The old zebra nodded.

"And the needles *do* hurt," she continued softly.

He nodded again.

"And . . . I guess I apologize all the time because I want everyone to like me," she confessed meekly.

"Well, you've failed!" Zilch sang out gleefully.

Xerxes shot Zilch a contemptuous look. "Fool," he spat.

"*Fool?*" Zilch echoed incredulously. "I'm the only zebra in this herd with a discernible brain!"

Xerxes' answer to Zilch was a nasty nip on his flank. Zilch yowled melodramatically and tried to stomp on Xerxes' hoof, but by mistake stomped on little Zero instead.

"Kwa!" Zero yelped painfully, limping away.

"You're so mean to each other!" Becky exclaimed.

"Play nice," Papa Zeke admonished the herd sharply. He turned back to Becky. "Thank you for telling me the truth. Also, my manners before were not so wonderful. I may have been a little harsh, so—"

"I'm sorry," Papa Zeke and Becky said together.

"Let's try that again," Papa Zeke suggested. "*I* have something to apologize for, and you . . . ?"

"Don't?" Becky ventured.

"Exactly!" Papa Zeke agreed. "I'm sorry. You're not. So enough with the apologizing and let's move on. Becky, we've planned a wonderful party in your honor. Zuzi will dance, the Z'bras will—"

"Eek!" Becky shrieked.

Something green and hairy had swung down from the tree to hang upside down in her face. "Hi!" the green thing said. Then it dropped to the ground and grinned up at her. Now Becky could see that it was a small, very odd-looking monkey.

"Wowee, Becky!" the monkey exclaimed, taking Becky's hand. "Your hand is in my paw. I mean my hoof. I'm zebra Shlep, just another member of the herd."

"Oh, please," Zilch groaned, "how utterly mortifying."

"Shlep isn't one of us," Zuzi confided.

"Am too," Shlep insisted. He scratched nervously under an arm and a tuft of green fur floated to the ground.

"You think you're a zebra?" Becky asked the monkey.

"Astonishing, isn't it?" Zilch asked. "He's so . . . green. And he has terrible monkey breath."

Shlep bounded over to Zilch. "I do not."

"Do too," Zilch jeered.

"Do not!"

"Do too!"

The entire herd took sides and began to quarrel, butting heads and kicking hooves for emphasis.

"Please, please stop fighting!" Becky cried. Slowly the herd quieted. "I'm sorry if I said the wrong thing."

"Again with the apologizing," Papa Zeke muttered.

"It's because I hate fighting," Becky explained. "My parents never used to fight, but today they had a terrible fight. It was all my fault. This is probably my fault too."

"Oh, no," Zuzi assured her, "zebras argue all the time."

"Humans argue, zebras argue." Papa Zeke shrugged. "I'm not saying it's wonderful, but it happens. You are not personally responsible."

Becky sagged against the tree. "Then why do I feel like I am?"

"Dr. Paula would say you lack self-esteem!" Zap chimed in from where she stood watch thirty yards away.

Papa Zeke winced. "Excuse her, she overhears too much shortwave talk radio. Now, about self-esteem. My great-grandmother of blessed memory—"

"May she rest in peace," the herd intoned.

"—used to tell me, 'Zekie, there's never enough self-esteem to go around. One day you got it and I don't, and one day I got it and you don't.' So the answer to your question is . . ."

"Yes?" the herd asked expectantly.

"I don't know," Papa Zeke concluded.

The herd groaned.

"And now, my zebra children, I invite you to take a load off your hooves and gather around our honored guest, namely Becky. It's time for the greatest story-teller of all time, namely me, to tell you a story."

Becky sat cross-legged under the tree, and the herd settled in around her. The little green monkey squeezed in by her side, gazing up at her with reverence.

She smiled at him. "I'm going to remember every single moment of this so I can tell . . ."

Who? she thought. Anyone she told would just say she had made it all up. It would have to be her secret forever and ever, written down in her secret journal.

Zuzi nuzzled Becky's arm. "Tell Papa Zeke we want to hear Zink," she urged.

"Zink! Zink! Zink!" the foals began to chant.

"What's Zink?" Becky asked.

"Yawn," Zilch said. "We've heard that story a zillion times."

"Becky hasn't heard the story, Mr. Rudeness," Papa

Zeke replied, then cleared his throat. "Zebra children, guest human, this is the story of Zink the zebra. Once upon a time there was a zebra—"

"Named Zink!" Zuzi interrupted eagerly.

"Named Zink," Papa Zeke repeated. "Now Zink was very different, because Zink had—"

"Polka dots instead of stripes!" Zuzi shouted.

"Polka dots instead of stripes." This time Papa Zeke was a bit irritated. "And all the other zebras—"

"Were very proud of their stripes!" Zuzi put in.

Papa Zeke glared at Zuzi. "Who's telling this story, missy?"

"Sorry." Zuzi meekly dropped her head to her forelegs.

"See, Becky?" Papa Zeke asked. "That time it really *was* her fault, and she apologized. That's how it works."

Becky nodded, and Papa Zeke nodded back.

"Now, where was I? Ah, yes. All the other zebras, who were very proud of their stripes—which meant they were part of the zebra herd—thought polka-dotted Zink was very strange and ugly. No one in the herd wanted to cavort with Zink. In fact, because Zink was so different, many even claimed that Zink—"

"—was not really a zebra at all," the herd intoned.

"Exactly," Papa Zeke concurred. "But one day during the rainy season, when the zebras were having a lovely frolic in the mud, they heard the roars of marauding lions."

"Predators," Becky said, her voice hushed. Already the Zink story seemed as real as if she had been there herself.

"Exactly." Papa Zeke's voice was hushed now too. "The zebras ran like lightning. But the roars of the lions grew louder, because they were faster than the zebras. They were ready to pounce on the zebras and eat them!"

Though the zebras knew the tale well, they still gasped.

"Then," Papa Zeke went on dramatically, "at the last possible moment, Zink, the polka-dotted zebra, broke away from the herd. Zink's unusual spots caught the attention of the lions, who turned away from the herd and began to chase after Zink instead!"

Becky had gotten so involved in the story that she hadn't felt Shlep clutch her hand with his green paw. "Did the lions eat Zink the zebra?" she asked fearfully.

"The zebras never saw Zink again," Papa Zeke finished solemnly. He fell silent, and the listening zebras looked very somber. No one spoke or even moved a muscle.

"I don't like that story," Becky finally said.

"However!" Papa Zeke continued suddenly, his face animated again. "My great-grandmother of blessed memory—"

"May she rest in peace," the herd intoned.

"—said she had a friend from another herd, Zaidey zebra, who had a sister who had a cousin by marriage, Zechariah zebra, who claimed he once drank dirty pond water next to a splendiferous polka-dotted zebra named Zink in another part of Africa, far, far away. However, this Zechariah zebra was a big liar. So the answer to your question is . . ."

"Yes?" Becky asked hopefully.

"I don't know," Papa Zeke concluded.

The herd groaned.

Becky stood up. "How can you not know? That's no way to end a story."

Papa Zeke shrugged as the other zebras stood up and began to graze. Xerxes and another big stallion went on watch, and the Z'bras rejoined the grazing herd.

Becky marched over to Papa Zeke. "Am I the only one who cares about what happened to Zink?" she demanded.

"Caring is a funny thing," Papa Zeke mused aloud. "Sometimes it shows, sometimes it doesn't. Sometimes you just change the subject."

Becky turned to Ice Z, who now stood near her

between Zip and Zap. "But why?" she asked in frustration. The lead stallion didn't answer. Instead, the three Z'bras opened their mouths and began to sing:

> *In the jungle, the mighty jungle, the lion sleeps tonight. . . .*

Becky was astonished. "That's my favorite song—the one I was going to sing in the talent show!"

> *In the jungle, the mighty jungle, the lion—*

Suddenly Ice Z stopped singing. His ears went back and he cautiously sniffed the air.

"What is it?" Becky asked, puzzled. "What?"

"Predators!" Ice Z bellowed just as Xerxes sounded the "Kwa-kwa!" alarm from his lookout.

"Go, Papa Zeke," Ice Z ordered, "get a head start!"

"What do I do?" Becky cried.

"Everyone, run with the herd!" Ice Z commanded. The zebras ran together toward the setting sun, a blur of black-and-white stripes.

"Wait! Please, don't leave me!" Becky ran after them, but it was useless. She couldn't keep up as the herd disappeared into the distance.

The roars of the lions grew louder. Becky dropped to

her knees. "I'm so scared," she whispered. "I'm so scared, I'm so scared, I'm so—"

"Becky! Becky! Up here!"

She looked up. Shlep was high in a baobab tree.

"Please help me!" she begged him.

The horrific roaring grew still louder. The lions were coming. Becky screamed in terror.

"Fly, Becky!" the monkey said. "Fly away!"

"I can't," Becky sobbed. "I don't know how to fly!"

Yes. You do. The voice had come from inside her head.

The lions pounded into view. They saw Becky. They charged.

That was when Becky remembered. She *did* know how to fly.

And just as the first lion pounced, Becky flew away.

CHAPTER NINE
The Warning

September 30

I can fly. I can leave my body. Zebras can talk. If you are
a big sneak who is reading this secret journal right now
without my permission, I AM ONLY JOKING. HA-HA.
DO NOT TURN THE PAGE. STOP READING
RIGHT NOW AND PUT MY JOURNAL RIGHT
BACK WHERE YOU FOUND IT OR I WILL BE
VERY MAD AT YOU FOREVER. I MEAN IT.

CHAPTER TEN

The Written-Down Truth

BECKY CHEWED the end of her pen as she read over the warning she had written, hoping that anyone who read it would actually put her journal down and not read it. Or if they did read it, they would think the whole thing was a big joke.

She sighed. Then she turned the page and wrote down every single thing that had happened the day before, from the moment the Z'bras showed up at the foot of her bed to the moment she flew away from the attacking lions. She knew it all sounded like some big made-up story, only it *wasn't* a made-up story. It was the truth.

When she was done and had read it all over to make sure she hadn't left anything out, she began to write again.

I was so HAPPY I remembered how to fly!!! I escaped from the lions, but I ended up back in the hospital, a place I did NOT want to be, which made me MAD and SAD at the same time. I am kind of scared about the leukemia but I am really, really scared about the herd!!! What if they didn't get away from the lions??? I will be worried until the Z'bras come back and say the herd is okay. I miss them already and I miss Shlep and most of all I miss Papa Zeke.

October 3

Good news!!! I got up the nerve to ask Mom what kind of cancer I have and she said ALL, which is the good kind of cancer, and she did not even know what Darlene told me so she can't be lying, which means I will live! I felt so happy that I joked around with Mom and Dad like we used to before I got sick. It made them happy to see me acting like my old self and that made me happy and they stopped being mad at each other and even held hands. For now things are good. Yeah!

October 4

Uh-oh. Darlene was just looking at me like I am such a baby because my mom is here almost all the time and her mom only drops off presents and leaves again. I hope Darlene is not a sneak because if she ever read my journal I would <u>die.</u> Mrs. Hudson came to see me and gave me a giant get-well card from my whole class, which Angela, the nice nurse, put up over my bed. Everyone signed it, even Ashley, who drew stars around her own name. She is so stuck-up. She would hate Angela because Angela has frizzy hair and is not skinny. Mrs. Hudson also gave me a book of poetry by Shaaban Robert, the national poet of Tanzania, but I am too tired to read it now. I wish the Z'bras would come back. I'm still getting chemo. I hate it here. I want to go home.

October 6

I have a problem and her name is Darlene. She thinks my mom treats me like a baby, like how Mom made a chart of my medicines and my schedule for taking them. So this morning, after my mom did the chart and went to the cafeteria, Darlene asked me if potty training was on my schedule and I was so embarrassed. Sometimes she is nice to me and we talk about stuff people who do not have cancer wouldn't understand but most of the time she is mean. Lee made me a get-well card. I miss him even though at home I think he is a pest. Angela, the nice nurse, is engaged but she didn't get her engagement ring yet. I miss the Z'bras. They are real and I know they will come back, I hope.

October 8

I feel very sick. Where are the Z'bras?

October 12

I was stupid to believe the Z'bras are real.

Chapter Eleven

AML, TBR, BMT

"BETTER?" Becky's mom asked. She gently put a cool, dampened washcloth on Becky's forehead.

Becky nodded. She slumped, exhausted, against the pillows. She'd been in the hospital for eighteen days now and had been throwing up from her chemotherapy for the past three.

As for the Z'bras, she'd stopped hoping they would come back, and it left her with an empty feeling in her heart. Maybe Darlene was right about her acting like a baby. After all, only a baby would believe that a dream about talking zebras and flying to Africa was true.

Throwing up was awful, but at least her mom was

there with her. Every single time she retched, her mom would use one hand to hold the metal basin for her and the other hand to hold back Becky's hair. Her Africa Day braids were long gone. Instead, her mom had tied her hair back with a ribbon that matched Becky's favorite pajamas.

Becky glanced over at Darlene. She was on her back, eyes closed and wig askew. Darlene was sick from her chemo too, but her mom was never around to help her. Usually Darlene refused to call the nurse and would hold the metal basin herself.

"Okay, sweetie, ready for another poem?" Mrs. Zaslow asked Becky. She opened the book of Shaaban Robert's poems to the bookmark and pulled her chair closer to Becky's bed.

> *Child, you may grasp this:*
> *That sparkles beget fire,*
> *The river begins as a rivulet,*
> *And a drop of water makes the lake and the ocean.*

"So did that guy write in English or in Swahili?" Darlene asked abruptly.

Becky was surprised that Darlene had been listening.

"Swahili," Mrs. Zaslow said. "This is a translation."

"The guy's dead, right? So the translator could have

totally wrecked this guy's work and he'd never even know it," Darlene said. "Look, can we stuff a sock in Culture Hour, please? I have to—"

Darlene didn't finish her sentence. Instead, she grabbed her metal basin and leaned over the side of the bed. The sound of her gagging made Becky feel sick herself.

"Would you like me to get the nurse for you, Darlene?" Mrs. Zaslow asked. She was always nice to Darlene, even though Becky could tell that her mom didn't like her much.

"No." Darlene retched again.

Mrs. Zaslow turned the cool cloth on Becky's forehead. "How are you doing, Becks?"

"Okay." Becky managed a small smile.

The door opened and Mrs. Dunbar peeked in, carrying a large, gift-wrapped box. "Oh, my poor baby!" she wailed when she saw her daughter throwing up. She hurried to Darlene's side, her high heels clicking across the linoleum. Mrs. Dunbar was all dressed up, just as she had been during her other rare visits to their room.

"Nice of her to join us," Mrs. Zaslow muttered.

"I hate this so much," Mrs. Dunbar sobbed, rummaging in her purse for a tissue. "I don't know what to do anymore."

Becky couldn't believe it. Darlene's mom didn't even try to help her own daughter!

Mrs. Dunbar blew her nose, then looked up at the ceiling. "I can't take much more of this, I really can't. I'll find someone to help you, honey." She walked to the door, then turned back. "The new jeans you wanted are in the box, okay?"

"Unbelievable," Mrs. Zaslow grumbled as Mrs. Dunbar headed down the hall to the nurses' station.

"I might be sick again, Mom," Becky whispered.

"Let's check how long it is until your Zofran, Becks."

Zofran was the antinausea medicine Becky was taking. Darlene was allergic to it and took something else. Mrs. Zaslow checked her watch, then her chart. She frowned.

"They're ten minutes late with it. Let me—"

The door opened and a short, thin nurse Becky had never seen before hurried in, carrying a tray with a little white paper cup on it.

"Hello," Mrs. Zaslow said. "Are you new?"

"I'm a floater," the nurse explained. "Three peds nurses are out with flu so it's a little crazy." She handed the cup to Becky and poured some water into Becky's glass.

"Just a minute," Mrs. Zaslow said, peering at the pill in the cup. "That's supposed to be Zofran."

"Right," the nurse said. She handed the pill to Becky.

"Don't take that pill, Becky," Mrs. Zaslow said sharply. She turned to the nurse. "It's not Zofran."

"Of course it is," the nurse said.

"No, it's not. I'm sorry, Ms."—Mrs. Zaslow peered at the nurse's name badge—"Owens. Zofran looks like a little football, and that pill is skinnier." She showed the nurse the chart she'd made, complete with colored-pencil drawings of each of Becky's pills.

Becky flushed with embarrassment. No one else's mother had a pill chart with drawings. She peeked at Darlene, hoping she was asleep, but Darlene was watching the proceedings with great interest.

"Maybe her doctor switched her to generic," the nurse said, failing to hide her irritation.

Mrs. Zaslow shook her head. "Double-check that medication. And please do it quickly, because my daughter has been throwing up for the last hour."

The nurse frowned. "Look, I can't leave this room until your daughter takes her pill. Do you know how many more kids are waiting for their meds right now?"

"I'm sure all of them want to take the *right* meds," Mrs. Zaslow said, staring her down. "And I'm sure that's what you want too."

Ms. Owens didn't waver. "Ma'am, I assure you this is the right medication," she said icily.

Mrs. Zaslow snatched the paper cup and dumped the pill into her right hand. She peered at it closely.

"This pill says Zoloft on it."

The nurse paled. "That's impossible."

"Read it." Mrs. Zaslow handed her the pill, and the nurse read it. Then she put it on her tray.

"The pharmacy fills the meds, we just deliver them," she said quickly. "Someone down there must have gotten Zofran mixed up with Zoloft. They're shorthanded because a lot of people are out with—"

"Guess what. I don't care," Mrs. Zaslow snapped. "There is no excuse for this."

"Mom—" Becky sat up. She was going to be sick again.

Her mother grabbed the metal basin. "It's okay, Becks," she said, holding back Becky's hair and eyeing the nurse at the same time. "Ms. Owens will be right back with your Zofran. *Right back.*"

The nurse turned on her heel and headed for the door.

"I'm sorry," Ms. Owens said over her shoulder. But Becky was too sick to care.

"OH, SUPER, it's Becky!" Ms. Bell, the play therapist, sang out as Becky wheeled her IV into the rec room. Ms.

Bell sat at a table with six little kids, cutting pumpkins out of orange paper. Wendy Barr, a three-year-old with brain cancer, sat on her lap, grinning. Wendy couldn't talk anymore, but she smiled all the time.

"Oh, super, it's Becky!" Darlene whined, imitating the therapist. She sat in front of the TV across the room with a boy Becky didn't know.

"It's Halloween tomorrow," Ms. Bell reminded Becky. "Want to make a pumpkin?"

Becky had mouth sores from her chemo and it hurt to talk, so she smiled and shook her head as she wheeled her IV over to Darlene and the boy. An old horror movie was on TV.

"Tinkerbell Bell over there is so sweet she gives me diabetes," Darlene said to the boy as Becky sat down.

Becky looked at him. He looked older than Darlene. He had dark eyes, a handsome face, and muscles in his arms. As he watched the movie, he curled a small hand weight with his right arm, over and over. Becky could see that he was bald under his baseball cap, which made her glad all over again that she hadn't lost her hair.

"I'm going to get the pumpkin for the jack-o'-lantern," Ms. Bell announced. "Everyone can help!"

"Stuff a sock in it, Tinkerbell," Darlene muttered as the boy switched the weight to his other hand. "Did you ever hear anything so utterly juvenile?"

Darlene had on a lot of black eyeliner, black pants, and platform boots. Her IV tube snaked under her T-shirt and hooked up with an indwelling catheter that tunneled into her chest. She was skinnier than ever and was being fed through the catheter because she couldn't keep solid food down.

When the boy didn't answer, Darlene turned to Becky as if she had just arrived. "Oh, hello, roomie, dear. This is Joe. Joe, this is sweet little Becky. Joe's fifteen," she added significantly.

Joe stood up and left.

"Right, catch you later," Darlene called after him.

"He's kind of rude," Becky whispered. Her mouth hurt.

"He happens to be very deep. Tonight's his last night of freedom. In the morning he gets TBR for a BMT."

"What?"

Darlene made a noise of disgust. "Since when is it my job to educate you about everything?"

"It isn't," Becky admitted softly.

Darlene rolled her eyes. "TBR is total body radiation which is like X rays only stronger and it kills off cancer cells because if you've got a lot of cancer cells you can't have a BMT, which is a bone marrow transplant, and if you have AML you have to get a BMT if you get a first remission or else you die. Got it?"

Becky didn't but nodded anyway.

"No, you don't," Darlene said. "You've got mouth sores, don't you? I *told* you to rinse with Magic Mouthwash so you wouldn't get 'em."

"Pat said to use it after I got sores, not before." Becky could barely croak the words out.

Darlene sighed. "Pat gave notice today to take a new job in California. Try to keep up. And let me ask you a question. Did *she* ever have mouth sores from chemo?"

Becky shook her head.

"So which one of us should you believe?" Darlene got up unsteadily and reached for her IV pole. "Come on. You can use some of my Magic Mouthwash till you can get a 'scrip from Franklin. Magic Mouthwash is the best."

They wheeled past Joe's room. His door was open, and Darlene waved to him. Joe didn't wave back. He just sat on his bed, expressionless, curling the dumbbell.

Darlene wheeled her IV inside his door. Becky didn't know whether she should go in too and decided to wait in the doorway.

"Listen, about your TBR," Darlene told him, her voice intense. "No matter how sick you get, don't call a nurse. If the nurse comes in they turn off the radiation, and the torture will last longer. Don't forget, okay? Okay?" She waited for him to answer, more upset than Becky had ever seen her.

Joe didn't look at Darlene, but finally he nodded.

"Okay." Darlene sounded relieved. "So I'll see you."

She wheeled her pole back into the hall, and Becky followed her to their room. When they got there, Darlene went into the bathroom and opened the medicine cabinet.

"His chances are good; his mom was his donor," Darlene went on as she took out her bottle of Magic Mouthwash and handed it to Becky. "TBR and BMTs are the worst. Here. Happy Halloween. I'm going back to the lounge."

After Darlene left, Becky poured some mouthwash into a cup and tried to gargle. It flew everywhere. Her mouth sores hurt. Everything hurt.

Last Halloween, she remembered, *my whole family went to the Bowders' big annual costume party. Mom was Minnie Mouse, Dad was Mickey Mouse, and Lee was a pirate. Sara and I were twin mermaids. Instead of Magic Mouthwash, I got all this candy.*

It was so much fun.

CHAPTER TWELVE

November

November 4

THE Z'BRAS ARE BACK!!! They said the whole herd escaped from the lions and I am <u>so happy!!!</u> I told them I am sorry I stopped believing they were real, but they said they aren't mad at me and they missed me as much as I missed them. Yeah!!! This is what happened. I had to have another spinal tap to see if there is cancer in my central nervous system. I had one last week and they HURT. Right before Dr. Franklin stuck that gigantic needle into my spine, I shut my eyes, and something told me to think about Zink. The next thing I knew, there were Ice Z, Zip, and Zap!!! We sang "The Lion Sleeps Tonight" through the whole thing, and afterwards everyone said what a good patient I was and what a good voice I have and all I could do was laugh.

November 6

Joe is in an isolation room with a sign on the door that says EXTREME CAUTION. He can't have visitors because any germ could kill him until the marrow from his BMT grafts. The doctors and nurses have to wear special masks when they see him. Angela says Joe is too depressed to talk or even eat. Darlene writes secret letters to him and slips them under his door. I wonder if he is her b.f. Angela still didn't get her engagement ring and she had a fight with her b.f. so the wedding might be O-F-F but I hope N-O-T!

November 14

Double good news. Joe is better and Angela's engagement is back on!!! She got the ring and SHE INVITED ME TO BE IN THE WEDDING!!! It will be next fall. I can be excited for ten whole months. Darlene and I will both be junior bridesmaids. Darlene said she will be very mad if she dies before Angela's wedding, ha-ha, but I didn't think it was funny. This will be my first wedding ever. ANGELA + PAUL = TRUE LOVE.

November 18

I got really sick this afternoon. Mom wasn't here and Darlene was down in X ray and Angela had the day off. I pushed the nurse button but she didn't come and finally I had to go in my bed, which was the worst thing ever, ever, ever. When a nurse did come she said there had been an emergency and then she changed my sheets. Mom asked did I want to wear adult diapers just in case of another accident? I got mad at her. If she had been here it would not have happened. I felt bad after that but I did not say sorry. Now I know that not saying sorry when it is your fault feels even worse than saying sorry when it is not your fault. But I am still mad and I will never, ever, ever, ever wear a D-I-A-P-E-R and I mean it. Signed REBECCA ROSE ZASLOW

November 19

The emergency yesterday is that Wendy died. I never knew anyone who died except my grandmother but I was only two then so I don't remember. Why should a little girl die? I feel so sad but Darlene shrugged like it was a big nothing. This afternoon her mom sent her a brand-new big-screen TV but she hasn't turned it on yet. Mom and Dad went to visit Wendy's parents and then they came to see me. Dad's eyes were red from crying but Mom's were not red and she said Wendy dying just made her mad. There is already a new girl in Wendy's room. She has bone cancer. It is so sad.

November 22

Today I had another blood transfusion. The blood looks gross in the plastic bag on my IV. The Z'bras came and I asked Ice Z why sometimes they come and sometimes they don't, but he didn't know. I asked him when I could go back to Africa and he didn't know that either. THIS IS VERY FRUSTRATING. I am sick of being sick. Ice Z says it is okay to let my feelings out but I don't except for that one time with Mom about the word that starts with a D and rhymes with wipers, ICK-ICK-ICK.

Oh, the new girl with bone cancer's name is Honora, isn't that pretty? It's her third relapse. Angela said Honora doesn't have a dad and the sicker Honora gets the less her mom comes to see her. When I heard that I hugged Mom so tight. I told the Z'bras I wished they could visit Honora so she wouldn't feel so lonely. But Zap said maybe she has her own zebras. I never thought of that.

November 25

I had ANOTHER spinal tap and it was bad but not too bad because the Z'bras made up dance steps to "The Lion Sleeps Tonight" and did them for me. I feel like I've been in this hospital forever. Sometimes I get scared that I'll never get better. Ice Z said to talk about that with my parents but I think it would scare them too much. Happy Thanksgiving. Ice Z said I should try to think of something good about every single day. My good thought for today is that I still have all my hair!!!

CHAPTER THIRTEEN

The Blizzard

BECKY COULDN'T WAIT to tell Darlene the good news. As soon as Darlene walked in the door from the rec room, where she'd been watching some high-school kids put on a Christmas play, she jumped off her bed and said, "Guess what."

"I don't want to guess what." Darlene lay down on her bed and closed her eyes.

"I'm going home," Becky announced. "Day after tomorrow. I'm cured."

"Maybe."

"I *am* cured," Becky insisted. "Dr. Franklin said I'm in remission."

"Cured means five *years* in remission. I don't think that applies to you."

"It won't come back."

Darlene looked over at her. "How do you know?"

"I just do," Becky insisted. "I thought you'd be happy for me. We're both better. We're both going home."

"I *am* happy for you," Darlene snapped. "Thrilled."

"You don't sound it."

"It just so happens that I'm not even thinking about you right now, okay? I just found out that Joe's got GVHD. And please don't ask me what that is."

Becky started to apologize but stopped herself. She wasn't going to do that anymore. Instead, she reached for the book her mom had brought her and started to read.

Darlene's voice interrupted her. "If you have to know, it's graft-versus-host disease."

"I didn't say anything," Becky protested.

"His donor cells are attacking his own body. He's got the rash. That's exactly how it started with Carolyn."

"Who's Carolyn?"

Darlene got under the covers and turned away from Becky. "Just leave me alone."

* * *

December 20

I have been home for three days. I am sad but I can't tell anyone because I am supposed to be happy. Nothing is how I thought it would be. First, Darlene wouldn't say good-bye to me. Then, when Dad brought me home, Lee went to hug me but Mom screamed at him not to touch me because of germs and he ran off crying. Mom tried to explain to him that even little germs like his cold germs could make me very sick right now but he is only six and thinks Mom meant that if he touched me he could catch my cancer. So now he won't come near me. Even though we tell him that cancer isn't catchy, he doesn't believe us. Mrs. Hudson wants to visit me and Sara's mom said she'd bring Sara over, but I can't have visitors yet because of stupid germs.

My face is all fat from chemo and I look ugly and I still feel so sick. I had to pretend to be happy when we got our Chanukah presents. What if I am not really in remission and my parents are lying to me? The only ones I could ask are the Z'bras, and they haven't been to see me since I left the hospital. I am so scared.

December 22

I feel so much better!!! It turns out that the reason I felt sick was from the IV chemo drugs still in my system but now I feel almost like the old me. HOORAY! I got new blood counts and they were very good so Mrs. Hudson is coming to visit. I am <u>so glad</u> I didn't tell my parents that I thought they were lying to me. Tonight Dad kissed the back of Mom's neck just because he was happy. I still miss the Z'bras but now that I'm better I don't miss them as much. Maybe they only know the way from Africa to the hospital. Ha-ha.

Mrs. Hudson sat on the couch in Becky's living room, looking through Becky's new cassette tapes. It was Saturday morning and there had been an overnight blizzard. Becky could hear the sound of her parents shoveling the driveway, and through the picture window she could see Lee on his back in the snow, waving his arms and legs to make snow angels.

Part of Becky wished she could be outside too. It was strange to have a teacher sitting on the living room couch, even if she was her favorite teacher, and to feel as if she had to be on school behavior instead of home behavior.

"You have the beginnings of an excellent musical library here," Mrs. Hudson told Becky. She lifted a tape to read the title. "The Space Bandits Band?"

Becky chuckled. "That one's from my brother. 'Superhero Sam and the Space Bandits' is his favorite television show. He runs around with a towel pinned around his neck, pretending he's Sam."

"I see." Mrs. Hudson smiled. She put the tape back

in the tape box and took out another. " 'The Lion Sleeps Tonight,' by the Tokens. I love that song! How does the funny part at the beginning go again?"

" 'Wimoweh, a-wimoweh, a-wimoweh,' " Becky sang softly.

Mrs. Hudson laughed. "That's it! I used to sing it on the school bus with my sister."

"It's what I wanted to sing in the talent contest," Becky confided shyly.

Mrs. Hudson put the tape back. "And why can't you still sing it?"

Becky shrugged. "I missed the auditions. Everyone else had to audition. They won't think it's fair."

They think. What do you think?

"Papa Zeke?" Becky jumped up. She was sure she had heard his voice. But where was he?

"Excuse me?" Mrs. Hudson asked.

Becky opened her mouth to tell Mrs. Hudson about Ice Z's herd, how she had flown to Africa to visit them and— No. It would sound as ridiculous as Lee insisting that a towel around his neck turned him into a super-hero.

"Nothing." Becky sat back down. "Sorry."

Mrs. Hudson's face grew stern. "Let me ask you a question. Do you think it's fair that you got cancer?"

"I don't know," Becky said.

"Do you think you got leukemia because you are mean, and your classmates didn't get it because they are nice?"

Becky shrugged. "I guess I don't think that."

"So then you will be in the talent contest."

"I want to," Becky said slowly. "But Ashley will be mad at me. Then she'll tell everyone else to be mad at me, and—"

"Ashley," Mrs. Hudson repeated. "Becky, my mother used to say *machoni rafiki, moyoni mnafiki*. It means 'friendly in the eyes, a hypocrite in the heart.' "

Becky nodded.

"So we agree," the teacher said. "When you come back to school, I will announce you are singing in the contest."

Back to school. The three scariest words in the English language, Becky thought.

"Do you think . . ." Becky hesitated. "When I come back to school, I want everyone to treat me normally."

"Certainly," Mrs. Hudson said emphatically. "Before vacation, Ms. Bingham put on an assembly about leukemia for the whole school, so no worries."

"They won't think they'll catch it from me?"

"Not at all."

Becky dug her thumbnail into the couch cushion. "I missed a lot of work. I thought I could do homework at the hospital, but lots of times I was too sick. I didn't even get to do South America. And you started on India before winter vacation, so—"

"Becky." Mrs. Hudson took her hand. "Missing schoolwork is not such a terrible thing."

Becky was dumbfounded. "But you're a teacher! How can you say that?"

Mrs. Hudson laughed. "I think you've had quite an education in the past couple of months." She patted Becky's hand. "Oh! I almost forgot. I brought you a Chanukah present of my own."

She reached into her large tote bag and took out something wrapped in gold tissue paper. "Go ahead," she said. "Open it."

Becky tore it open. Inside, folded up, was some soft, beautiful material, as orange as a Serengeti sunset.

"Shake it out," Mrs. Hudson urged. "It's a sari, the traditional dress for women in India." She motioned for Becky to stand up, then deftly draped the sari over Becky's jeans and sweater, looped it over one of her shoulders, and tucked in the end securely.

Becky went to the hallway mirror to see how she looked, her teacher following her. "It's beautiful," Becky marveled, turning to and fro in front of her reflection. Then she frowned. "But my face is fat and ugly from chemo."

Mrs. Hudson gently turned Becky toward her. "Shall I tell you about my beautiful sister? She had a kidney tumor when she was sixteen."

"She did?"

Mrs. Hudson nodded. "Her medicine also made her face rounder for a time, and she cried about it. But do you know? She was still chosen the most beautiful girl in her school."

Becky looked skeptical. "Is that true?"

Mrs. Hudson's eyebrows went up. "Do you believe I would say it was true if it was not?"

Becky thought a moment. "No," she finally said. She turned back to her reflection.

Ugh. No one would ever choose me as most beautiful.

"You have lovely hair," Mrs. Hudson said. "Young girls in India wear their hair in a long braid down their backs. Shall I show you? Do you have a brush and an elastic?"

Becky got them from her room and brought them back to Mrs. Hudson. Then she stood before the mirror again and tilted her head a little. She tried out a smile.

Maybe I don't look all that ugly, she thought.

"Most Indians are Hindu," Mrs. Hudson explained as she brushed Becky's hair. "Hindus believe that some animals are sacred, such as the cow, so in the streets of—"

Becky gasped. A huge hank of her hair had just come off in Mrs. Hudson's hand.

"Oh, Becky," Mrs. Hudson whispered sadly.

Becky whirled around and snatched the hair from her teacher.

"I'm so sorry," Mrs. Hudson said. "But it will grow back. You must see this as a badge of honor."

"Did your sister lose hers?" Becky demanded.

"Yes."

"Before or after she was picked as most beautiful?"

Mrs. Hudson's gaze didn't waver. "After," she said.

Becky let the hank of her hair drop to the ground, took the brush, and began to brush her hair. Her face was expressionless.

Hair fell everywhere.

"Do you want me to get your mother, Becky?"

"No. I'm fine. I just want to get this over with."

Becky brushed harder and harder, until hair covered the floor around her like a blanket of dirty snow.

CHAPTER FOURTEEN

Back to School

BECKY STARED OUT the car window as her mom drove the familiar route to Briarly Middle School. It was the first day after winter vacation, her first day back since cancer.

Her mother glanced at her. "Now, remember, if you get tired, just call me at—"

"The bookstore, I know." The closer they got to school, the more nervous she felt. She flipped down the sun visor on her side to look at herself in the mirror. Her face was still fat from the chemo drugs, and even though her wig was supposed to look just like her own hair, Becky knew it didn't. The color wasn't exactly the same, and the bangs were wrong too. She pushed it farther down on her head.

"How does that look?" Becky asked anxiously.

"Like a dead animal is sitting on your head," Lee offered from the backseat.

"Lee!" their mother admonished as she pulled the car up in front of Briarly. She turned to Becky. "It looks fine, Becks."

"No, it doesn't." Becky watched the kids streaming off the buses and running into the building. They all looked normal.

"You have your lunch money?"

Becky nodded, but she didn't open the door.

"Becks? Sweetie? Are you okay?" her mom asked softly.

"I'm fine."

"Just call me if you—"

"I'm *fine*. Thanks for the ride, Mom." Becky got out of the car, took a deep breath, and walked to the front door.

Down the hallway she walked. Everyone's eyes were on her, the alien who had just landed on planet Earth. She walked into Mrs. Hudson's classroom. Every head turned. Total silence.

"You're late, Becky," Mrs. Hudson finally admonished, just as she would have on any normal school day. "Have a seat quickly so we can get started."

"Sorry," Becky mumbled, sliding into her seat. She wished everyone would stop staring. She wished she could disappear.

As Mrs. Hudson took attendance, someone tapped her on the shoulder. It was Sara Bowder, who sat behind her. "I'm glad you're back," Sara said.

"Me too," Channa Gold whispered.

After that, Becky felt a little better.

BUT BY LUNCHTIME she was exhausted. She'd been told she could lie down in the nurse's office at any time, but she didn't want to be the only one in the entire sixth grade who needed a *nap*. So she dragged herself to the cafeteria and got in line behind Sara, Channa, and Ashley.

Dr. Franklin had explained to her that she wasn't really fat, just temporarily bloated from chemo, and it was critical for her to eat a nutritious lunch every day. Becky reached for a plate of spaghetti.

"Hey, you don't need that, porky!" a big eighth-grader yelled to her as he ran by, laughing.

She froze.

"You idiot!" Channa Gold shouted at him.

"She's not fat, she has *cancer*!" Ashley yelled even more loudly. Then, as soon as she saw that everyone was looking, she made a big show of putting her arm around Becky's shoulders as if they were best friends.

"Just ignore him, Becky," Channa advised.

Becky felt pinned to the spot where she stood, like the bugs they'd examined under the microscope in science class. A fat, ugly cancer bug.

"Come and sit with me and Sara and Channa," Ashley told Becky. "Want me to carry your tray?"

Becky forced herself to speak. "I can carry it." She picked up her tray. They found an empty table and sat down.

"So, you're all better now, right?" Channa asked.

Becky nodded.

Sara sipped her milk and smiled. "I'm so glad."

"I was *so* worried about you," Ashley said.

Machoni rafiki, moyoni mnafiki, Becky thought.

Ashley took a bite of her sandwich. "Was being in the hospital the most horrible thing in the world?"

Becky shrugged and pushed her spaghetti around.

"Did you know kids who actually died?" Ashley pressed.

Wendy Barr, Becky thought. *She was three. She had the sweetest smile. You don't deserve to know about her.*

Becky shrugged again.

"Maybe Becky doesn't want to talk about it," Channa said quickly. "Let's talk about something else."

"Hey, I just thought of something!" Sara exclaimed. "Now that you're better, you can be in the talent contest."

Becky blushed, because Mrs. Hudson hadn't yet announced that she was going to sing in the contest even though she hadn't auditioned.

"No, she can't, she didn't audition," Ashley said.

"So?" Channa asked. "She was in the hospital."

"*So?*" Ashley echoed. "She still didn't audition."

Becky bit her lip nervously. "Mrs. Hudson said I could still be in it. I'm—" She stopped herself from saying "sorry." She wasn't sorry, and she wasn't going to say it.

"Hudson's letting you be in the contest because she feels sorry for you," Ashley said sweetly. She got up and walked around the table to stand behind Becky. "We all do. Here. Let me return your tray for you, Becky."

"I can do it—" Becky began.

But Ashley was already reaching for it. Her arm jostled the back of Becky's wig and pushed it down Becky's forehead. "Oh, I'm sorry!" Ashley cried.

Becky pulled the wig back into place, her face burning with humiliation. Then she mumbled something about going to her locker and fled from the cafeteria, down the hallway, anyplace that was not someplace where she was so different from everyone else.

"Wait! Becky, wait!"

Becky turned around. Sara ran up to her, breathless.

"What?" Becky asked.

"I just wanted to say . . . Ashley can be really mean."

"Why are you friends with her, then?"

"She's the most popular girl in our whole grade."

"Maybe that's because everyone's afraid of her," Becky said. "You're afraid of her. Aren't you?"

Sara pushed her hair behind her ear. "Aren't you?"

Becky thought a moment. "There are things to be afraid of, Sara. But Ashley Chaffin isn't one of them."

Sara didn't look convinced. "Well, I just wanted to say I'm glad you're going to be in the talent contest."

"Thanks." Becky started to turn away.

"And I wanted to say one more thing too," Sara added.

Becky turned back to her. "What?"

Sara grinned. "I hope you beat her."

CHAPTER FIFTEEN

Happy Birthday

February 18

I haven't written for a long time. Sorry!!! Tomorrow I turn
eleven, HAPPY BIRTHDAY TO ME. Everything is
good. My hair is still too short so I wear my (gag!) wig, but
my face isn't fat anymore and I look almost like my normal
self. Sara is my friend again, almost like before she got to
be friends with that liar Ashley. Darlene was right about
how terrible liars are. Even though she didn't like me I
think about her sometimes, and also Joe and Honora and
all the other kids. I could call Angela and she'd tell me how
they are, but I never do. She must be planning her wedding
now. I don't care about being in it anymore. She only asked
me because I was sick and I'm not sick anymore and I AM

GLAD. My blood counts are so good that I don't have to worry about germs, which means tomorrow for my birthday Sara can come over for dinner and a sleepover. FUN!!! I am so-o-o glad we're best friends again. Sara said Ashley tells everyone the only reason I'm in the talent contest is because my mom called Mrs. Hudson and cried. That made me mad. I hate liars and I hate mean people and I HATE ASHLEY CHAFFIN!!!

Becky held her left wrist up to her bedroom mirror. On it was Sara's birthday present to her: a silver bracelet with a music note hanging from it. "I love it," she'd just told Sara, beaming.

What she hated was how the mirror reflected her stupid wig. She didn't usually wear it at home with her family, but Sara wasn't family. Still, she *was* Becky's best friend.

"Sara, I want to show you something," Becky said. "But you have to promise not to laugh."

"Promise." Sara plopped down on Becky's bed.

Becky hesitated. "My hair is still really short."

Sara shrugged. "It'll grow."

Becky pulled off her wig. Her hair was barely an inch long, darker and curlier than it had been before chemo. She felt terribly self-conscious. To cover, she struck a Darlene-type dramatic pose. "Well? Be brutal."

"It's kind of cute," Sara decided.

Becky flushed with happiness. "Really?"

Sara nodded. "I saw a model with her hair like that."

Becky grinned and took a running leap onto her bed. "I'm never, ever cutting it again. I'm letting it grow until it reaches the floor."

"*Longer* than the floor," Sara said. "You can wrap it around your head in a swirlie like my dad does to cover his bald spot."

"That's mean," Becky said, conking Sara on the head with her toy zebra. They both laughed.

Becky balanced the zebra on her raised knees, which made her think about the Z'bras. They hadn't come since she'd left the hospital. The more time that passed, the less real they seemed.

"Sara, did you ever have a dream that seemed so real you thought it *was* real?"

"Let's see," Sara mused. "Once I dreamed I took my coat off at school and underneath I was totally naked."

Both girls shuddered in horror.

"But not like that," Becky said. "I mean like . . . like a whole other world."

Sara scrunched up her nose. "Like science fiction?"

"Never mind," Becky said softly. She put her toy zebra under her pillow.

Sara sat up. "So, let's hear your song for the talent contest. Have you been practicing?"

"It's not very good."

"Ashley's lip-synching instead of singing because she knows your voice is way better than hers," Sara reported. "Her mom paid her dance teacher to make up her dance, and they ordered this sequined costume from New York."

"I don't have a costume," Becky said.

Sara shrugged. "You don't need one, you have talent."

Becky made a face. "Can you believe my secret dream is to become a famous singer and I'm too scared to sing in the talent contest?"

"Hee-yah!" Becky's door flew open from one of Lee's karate kicks. He wore red long underwear and a towel pinned around his shoulders. "I'm Superhero Sam, and I save the day!" he sang lustily.

"We're busy," Becky said. She got up to shut the door.

Lee put his hands on his hips and stepped into the room. "But Superhero—"

"Want to hear Becky sing?" Sara asked him.

"Hee-yah!" Lee yelled. He did a dive somersault onto Becky's floor, sprang to his feet, and launched himself into his sister's arms. He hugged her a lot now, his fear of touching her long forgotten.

Becky hugged him back. He was very cute. "I can't sing in front of both of you, though."

"But you're going to sing in front of the whole school at the contest," Sara pointed out. "And all the parents and guests and . . ."

Becky leaned against the wall. "Ugh. I feel sick just thinking about it."

"Yeah, but not *really* sick like before," Lee said anxiously. "Right?"

"Right," Becky assured him.

He gave her a smug look. "I knew it. Superhero Sam saves the day!" he bellowed.

"Hey, Superhero Sam, come help me put the laundry away," Mrs. Zaslow called.

"Why can't Becky help?" Lee hollered back.

"Because it's her birthday and she has a friend over!" Mrs. Zaslow appeared in the doorway holding a full laundry basket. "Move it, Lee."

Lee dived onto Becky's bed. "It's not fair. I had to do everything when she was sick, so now she should have to do everything."

"Just be glad it's over." Mrs. Zaslow put down the basket. "Sometimes I'd like to forget the whole thing even happened," she admitted. "Wouldn't you, Becks?"

The worst experiences can offer the best lessons, Becky. But not if you forget to remember them.

"Papa Zeke?"

It *had* been his voice, she was *sure* of it. Becky whirled around hopefully, looking for him.

"Papa *who?*" Lee asked. Sara and Mrs. Zaslow stared at Becky as if she had lost her mind.

"I guess it was the TV downstairs," Becky mumbled.

Mrs. Zaslow didn't look convinced, but she let it go. "Dad's bringing home ice cream for the birthday cake," she said. "What flavor do you guys want?"

"Strawberry." Becky sat, heavy with disappointment. She was sure she had heard Papa Zeke.

"Superhero Sam likes chocolate marshmallow!" Lee ordered, bouncing up and down.

"Superhero Sam can get out of my room now," Becky said.

Lee clomped to the door, then turned back to Becky. "I hated it when you were in that hospital." He ran out of the room, pulling their mother behind him.

Sara drew her knees up and rested her chin on them. "It must have been really scary to be in the hospital."

Becky nodded. "Way scarier than the talent contest."

Sara playfully kicked Becky. "So that means you can do it, then!" She reached for Becky's hairbrush on the nightstand and scrambled up onto the bed.

"And now, ladies and gentlemen," she announced

into the hairbrush, "I give you the soon-to-be-famous singer who is way more talented than Ashley Chaffin . . . Becky Zaslow!" She tossed the brush to Becky.

Becky lifted it to her mouth. She *could* do it.

She closed her eyes and began to sing.

CHAPTER SIXTEEN

The Dry Season

FOR MANY MONTHS, Ice Z's herd had migrated toward the Mara River. And for just as many months, Shlep had been depressed. He had failed his own zebra test.

Back in the autumn, when the herd had been about to cross the river, Shlep had been determined that, this time, he would swim the Mara like all the other zebras.

Crossing day had come, and Shlep had stood on the riverbank, a tiny splotch of green in an undulating, black-and-white wave. All around him, thousands of zebras were jumping into the water and thrashing their way to the other side.

Just as Ice Z had been about to lead his herd across,

a colt from another zebra herd lost his balance. As he was swept helplessly downriver to the waiting crocodiles, he had looked forlornly into Shlep's eyes.

Shlep immediately jumped onto Ice Z's back, grabbed Ice Z's mane for dear life, and slammed his eyes shut. He didn't open them again until Ice Z had swum to the far bank.

The monkey had done his best since then to forget that day, but truly forgetting was impossible. Because a river crossed in one direction must someday be crossed in the other. There was a cycle to things. The dry season led to the rainy season, but the dry season always came again. Things were born, things died.

It was the way it was.

The days were blistering, the air thick with dust and hungry sweat bees. Ice Z's herd had to range far to feed, which emboldened the lions to attack. Each day's travel meant passing the bones of recently devoured animals. And the time to cross the Mara was coming again.

The zebras and Shlep were in an awful mood.

"HEY!" Zilch bumped hard into Zuzi, who had just bitten off a dusty mouthful of grass. "What do you think you're doing? I was about to graze right here."

"It doesn't have your name on it, Zilch."

Zilch used his body to push Zuzi aside, but Zuzi stuck her head under him and polished off the last of the grass.

"You warthog," Zilch barked. "You steal everyone's fair share."

Zuzi fluttered her eyelashes angrily. "I do not."

Zilch struck an imperious pose. "Oh no? Then how is it that it's the dry season and you're *fat*?"

"Lose thirty pounds in thirty days, ask me how!" Zap called out from where she stood on watch.

"Would you please shut up with those insufferable radio commercials?" Zilch yelled. Then he yelped in pain as Zuzi stomped on his left front hoof.

"*That's* for calling me a warthog, you stinky hyena."

"Did I say warthog?" Zilch asked. "I meant *hippo!*"

She nipped at his flank and he butted her. The herd took sides, and within seconds all the zebras were calling each other names and kicking each other's flanks; Shlep scrambled away so he wouldn't be stepped on. The din grew loud enough to wake Papa Zeke from a nap.

"Enough argufying!" he growled grumpily. "Is a little peace and quiet so an old zebra can nap too much to ask?"

"We're bored." Zuzi pouted. "Tell us a story."

"Please spare us," Zilch groaned, swishing his tail

with annoyance. "If I hear 'Zink the zebra' once more I will be physically ill."

"Shut up, Zilch," Zuzi snapped.

Zip and Zap nodded in agreement. "We love Zink."

"A polka-dotted zebra named Zink?" Zilch asked, his tone withering. "It's almost as ludicrous as a green monkey named Shlep."

Shlep jutted out his chin. "I'm a zebra."

"I am so sick of all of you!" Zilch bellowed. He whirled around. "It's always the same thing with this herd, day in, day out. Look for food. Look for water. Listen to stories we've heard a zillion times. Watch for predators. Run from predators. And worst of all, put up with that stupid monkey!"

"Watch your tone, mister," Papa Zeke warned Zilch.

"I don't *want* to watch my tone, you ridiculous old zebra!" Zilch roared.

The herd gasped. Zip and Zap went to stand protectively by Papa Zeke as Ice Z walked slowly over to Zilch. Instinctively the herd formed a circle around the two of them.

"I think you need to calm down," Ice Z said.

Zilch's nostrils flared angrily. "What if I don't want to calm down?"

Ice Z's eyes narrowed. "Are you calling me out, Zilch? Because if you are, let's get it on."

Rhonda the sweat bee buzzed near Zilch's head. He shook her off. Then he turned sharply and trotted a few steps away.

He had broken.

There was an audible sigh of relief from the herd, and then one loud bark of derisive laughter. It was Xerxes, who had been standing off to one side, watching.

"I knew you'd never fight Ice Z for the herd," he told Zilch. Then he turned to Ice Z, a mocking sneer on his face. "Why don't you pick on a real zebra, Brother Ice?"

Ice Z walked deliberately over to the scarred zebra. "Do you have a problem, Xerxes?"

Xerxes stared him down. "Yeah, I imagine I do. With *you.*"

The herd oohed, and the circle re-formed around Ice Z and Xerxes. Shlep ducked in under Zip's belly, where he felt safer. The two massive stallions circled each other, Xerxes baring his teeth. But Ice Z didn't flinch.

"It's your call, Brother Xerxes," Ice Z said softly. "I don't want to fight you. But if I have to, I will."

"Is that right?" Xerxes asked. He kicked one hoof into the dust. "Because I'm thinking this herd needs a change."

The two stallions edged closer, breathing hard.

Rhonda and her band of bees hovered above them, anticipating mortal combat and, perhaps, a feast.

Ice Z stopped moving. "Say the word, then, Xerxes."

"You see that, Brother Ice?" Xerxes asked, cocking his head at the jagged scar on his neck. "I didn't live through *that* so I could listen to you give me orders all day. You want the word, Brother Ice? The word is . . . I'm leaving."

Rhonda and the sweat bees buzzed in disappointed shock. Then they sped off to spread the news as the circle of zebras looked at each other uncertainly.

"What, you were afraid I would beat him and be your new lead stallion?" Xerxes asked, looking from zebra to zebra, his lips curled in a cynical smile. "I want my own mare and my own herd. Not his leftovers."

He took a step forward and spit in Ice Z's face.

Infuriated, Ice Z rushed at the scarred zebra, who reared up on his hind legs. But instead of striking at Ice Z with a flying hoof, Xerxes *kwa*'d loudly, pushed off, and galloped away. The zebra circle parted to let him out. Ice Z chased him for several hundred yards, until it was clear Xerxes really was gone for good. Then he trotted back to his herd.

"Whew." Shlep rolled out from underneath Zip and sighed with relief.

"*Now* what is there to do?" Zuzi whined.

"That wasn't enough?" Shlep asked.

"You could gallop off into the sunset with Xerxes," Zilch suggested nastily. "Take the monkey."

Papa Zeke yawned. "Napping is an idea." His eyelids began to droop.

"I don't get it," Shlep said. "Aren't you guys upset about what just happened?"

"This is how zebras are, Shlepper," Papa Zeke said.

"Excuse me, Papa Zeke?" Zap asked timidly.

He opened his eyes. "Yes, Zap, what is it?"

"Papa Zeke, we miss Becky. We want her to come back."

The herd nodded in agreement.

"Traveling from one world to another is a difficult thing, my zebra children," Papa Zeke said. "It takes imagination, heart, and spirit. And most of all, wisdom."

"Becky has all those things," Zip said. "So why doesn't she come back to us?"

"As my great-grandmother of blessed memory used to say—"

"May she rest in peace," the herd intoned.

"—there's never enough wisdom to go around. One day you know everything and I don't, the next day I know everything and you don't, the third day we both see that we know nothing and start all over again trying to know something. So the answer to your question is . . ."

"Yes?" the zebras asked wearily.

"I don't know," Papa Zeke concluded.

The herd groaned and began to argue again.

Ice Z *kwa*'d sharply over the noise. "Listen up! We need to conserve our energy. I don't have to tell you that the next months are going to be tough. The lions will strike from one side, the hyenas will attack from the other. And eventually, we're going to have to cross that river again. The only question is when."

The argument started anew. Some wanted to make a mad dash for the Mara now, while others, more afraid of the river than of the lions, wanted to stay where they were. Two or three zebras even grumbled that Xerxes would have figured out a better plan than Ice Z, and maybe they had the wrong lead stallion after all.

Hooves flailed and tempers flared until finally Papa Zeke could take no more.

"So much fighting with your own family," Papa Zeke said. "You sadden me, my zebras." Then, with Shlep on his back, he trudged away to find a quiet place to sleep.

CHAPTER SEVENTEEN
Vacation

NO ONE'S STARING, Becky marveled as she walked with her family through the entrance area of the huge water-rides amusement park. *I'm wearing a bathing suit and a T-shirt and no one can tell I had cancer. If it wasn't for my short hair, I couldn't even tell my—*

"Race ya!" Lee started running. "Last one to the giant slide is a rotten egg!"

"That'll be you!" Becky laughed and ran after him.

"Save us a place!" their father called. He and their mom strolled behind them, arms around each other's waists.

It was March, and the Zaslows were on a family vacation in Florida. The night before they'd gone to a fantastic magic show. When the magician had asked for a volunteer for his final trick, Becky's hand had shot into the air, but a girl who looked kind of like Ashley Chaffin got picked. Becky barely cared. She was so happy just to be *normal.*

Becky easily ran past Lee. "No fair, your legs are longer!" he yelled.

She slowed down and joined the line for the slide. When Lee ran up to her, she yawned hugely. "Gee, what took you so long? I've been here for hours."

"Have not." He gaped at the giant slide, which was billed as the biggest in the world. "Wow. That's big!"

The two of them watched some teenage girls, high above them at the top of the slide. When they jumped on, they immediately started screaming.

"They're scared, huh?" Lee hitched up his swimsuit.

"I guess."

"Not me," he said, but his eyes were huge.

The line moved forward, and Becky saw the sign outside the big elevator that took twenty people at a time to the top. YOU MUST BE THIS TALL TO GO ON THE GIANT SLIDE. Lee was definitely not that tall. "Uh-oh," Becky muttered.

"What?"

Becky cocked her head at the sign. "You can read."

Lee stared at the sign. He knew his letters, but he wasn't a good reader the way Becky had been when she was six.

"So, I don't even care what it says," Lee told her.

"It says you're too little." She took his hand and led him out of line just as their parents caught up to them. "He's not big enough," Becky explained.

"Aw, I'm sorry, sport," Mr. Zaslow said.

"But it's not fair," Lee wailed.

"There's a kiddie slide and pool that way," a girl in a park uniform told them. "Down by the big pool."

"Thanks," Mrs. Zaslow told her.

Lee's face turned bright red. "A *kiddie* slide?"

Becky groaned. He could be such a pain. "Come on, I'll go with you."

"We'll buy you two some sodas and meet you there," their father suggested. "Okay, sport?"

"No," Lee said, but he walked there anyway with Becky. The kiddie slide was tiny. Lee glared at it as toddlers still in diapers slid down in their parents' arms.

"You want to give it a try?" Becky asked.

"No." Lee scowled. "I know what I shoulda done. I shoulda said I just got over cancer. Then I bet they woulda let me go on the giant slide."

"You can't lie like that," Becky told him.

"Why not?" he asked petulantly. "If you'd told 'em at the magic show you just got over cancer I bet they woulda picked you for that trick. If you get cancer, you get anything you want."

"Lee, it's horrible to have cancer."

He shrugged. "Mom was with you all the time and you got cards and presents and everything. You got better."

"That's mean."

"Who cares?"

What a brat! She was about to get really mad at him when she stopped herself. She wasn't six, he was.

"I'm sorry you couldn't go on the big slide," she told him. "I hate it when I can't do something I really, really want to do."

"Yeah, but I can't do *anything,*" Lee said. "I hate being the littlest."

"You won't be little forever," Becky told him. "Want to see who can make a bigger cannonball in the pool?"

"Yeah!" Lee shouted. He and Becky were both good swimmers. Together they ran to the edge of the big pool, launched themselves high into the air, and grabbed their knees. *Splash!* They hit the water at the same time.

When they popped up, they heard their mother

squealing with laughter at the other side of the pool. Their father had her in his arms, about to dump her in.

"What do you say, cannonballers?" he asked. "Yes or no?"

"Yes!" Lee yelled, a grin spreading over his face.

"Yes!" Becky cheered.

"You'll all pay for this!" their mom warned, but she was laughing so hard she could hardly get the words out.

Mr. Zaslow dropped his wife into the pool.

She came up sputtering and laughing, and Mr. Zaslow dived in after her. And right then, Becky knew just what she'd write in her secret journal when she got back to the hotel.

Today was better than perfect. It was normal.

"YOU KNOW, you look good like this," Becky told her father as she packed some more sand around his shoulders. It was a few days later; she and Lee were burying their father in the sand on the beach outside their hotel.

"Hey, if we bury him really deep, we can't leave

tomorrow," Lee pointed out hopefully. He dumped a bucket of sand on his father's stomach.

"Good try, kid." Mrs. Zaslow laughed, then looked at Becky. "It's been the best vacation ever, though, huh?"

"The best," Becky agreed. She was careful to fix a bright smile on her face.

"Can we get hamburgers for lunch and eat on the beach, please-please-please?" Lee asked.

Mr. Zaslow groaned playfully. "Where do you put it? You ate your breakfast *and* Becky's breakfast an hour ago."

Lee shrugged. "She wasn't hungry."

Becky got up and picked up her beach bag. "I have to go use the bathroom."

"Want me to come with, Becks?" her mom asked.

"No, stay and bury Dad. I can go myself."

Becky trudged off the beach, washed the sand off her feet, and entered the cool lobby of the hotel. A bellman smiled at her and she smiled back. She went to the bank of pay phones and took her little address book out of her beach bag to look up a number. Then she used her parents' calling card and dialed it.

"Miss Dunbar's residence," a British voice answered.

"Is Darlene there?" Becky asked.

"Whom shall I say is calling?"

"Becky Zaslow."

"Oh, hi, it's me," Darlene admitted, minus the accent.

"I thought maybe you told your parents to get you a butler and they did," Becky joked nervously.

"I wish. Now that I'm healthy, guilt-jerks don't work anymore. So what's up?"

"Nothing," Becky said, trying to sound casual. "How are you?" She scanned the lobby for her parents.

"I took a lickin' and kept on tickin'," Darlene said. "I'm the poster girl for beating Hodgkin's."

Becky licked her lips nervously. "That's great."

"Yeah. And I have two boyfriends. One's in high school. He thinks I'm fifteen."

"That's nice," Becky said.

Silence.

"So, you're okay?" Darlene asked.

"Great. I turned eleven."

More silence.

"Look," Darlene finally said, "I could make up some big lie about how I have to go and how it was great talking to you and all that, but you know how I hate liars so I'll just cut to the chase. Don't call me anymore."

Becky's throat tightened. "Oh. Okay."

"And you shouldn't *want* to call me either," Darlene went on. "The only thing we had in common doesn't exist anymore. So God bless, have a swell life, and good—"

"Wait! Don't hang up!" Becky clutched the phone. "I'm sorry, but . . . could I just ask you one thing first?"

"What?"

"Well, when you had a relapse, what happened?"

"You know what happened," Darlene said. "I went back to the stupid hospital, and—"

"No, I mean . . . how did you know you were having one?"

"I read it in a fortune cookie, what do you think?"

"Seriously," Becky pressed.

Darlene sighed. "The usual—fatigue, headaches, night sweats, no appetite—"

A teenage boy stood near Becky, waiting to use the phone. Becky turned her back to him. "But that could just be the flu, right?" she asked, her voice low.

"Please. I think I know the difference between the flu and . . . wait. You're having a relapse, aren't you?" Darlene accused.

"Probably not. I felt fine until yesterday."

"Tell me your symptoms," Darlene demanded.

"I'm not hungry," Becky forced herself to say, her

voice shaking. "I feel nauseous. I could hardly get out of bed this morning. And there's a bruise on my thigh—"

"Relapse," Darlene pronounced flatly.

The phone shook in Becky's hand. "Maybe not."

"Maybe you're stupider than I thought," Darlene said harshly. "Anyway, tell your parents, not me."

"But I don't want to worry them if—"

"Love ya, mean it," Darlene interrupted. "Look at the time, gotta run." The line went dead in Becky's hand.

There was a noise behind Becky. She hung up and took a deep breath to calm herself down. "You can use the phone now—"

She turned around, but the boy was no longer there.

Her father was, tears streaming down his cheeks.

He had heard everything.

No, no, no, no. It couldn't be happening. But it was.

He put his arms around her. "Oh, Becks, why didn't you tell us?"

"I thought it was the flu." She buried her head against his chest.

"Let me take you upstairs. Then I'll tell your mom. We need to call Dr. Franklin and get home right away."

She looked at him; it seemed as if he had aged twenty

years in the past few minutes. "I'm sorry, Daddy," Becky said. "I'm so sorry I made you cry."

He walked her to the elevator and back up to their room. Then he gave her a big hug and went back to the beach to get her mom and Lee.

Becky sat on the bed. She hugged her knees to her chest but still felt as if she were falling apart. "Ice Z?" she whispered. "Zip? Zap?"

She waited. Nothing happened.

"I'm sorry I haven't been a better friend," she said. "Please give me another chance. I'm so scared. Please come. Please?"

She waited again, hoping. But there was no answer.

CHAPTER EIGHTEEN

The Relapse

March 27

It's not fair, it's not fair, it's NOT FAIR. I am having a relapse and back in the hospital. My white count is over 200,000. Dr. Franklin said that 10,000 is normal and the rest are cancer cells, which is very, very bad. I am having chemo with different drugs that make me even sicker than the other ones. Probably all my hair will fall out and my face will get fat again just when I finally looked normal. Ms. Bell brought a girl puppet to me and asked me how the puppet felt about her relapse. I wanted to tell her what a stupid question that was but I just said "fine," only I said it in a sarcastic way like Darlene would. I am mad at everyone. I only say how I really feel here in my journal and to the Z'bras, but if the Z'bras don't come to see me soon I will be mad at them too, and I don't even care if no one likes me. I mean it. My feelings are the only private thing I have left.

April 6

I got a lot of antibiotics and I feel better. Joe is back. He was home in February but he got a bad infection. I walked past his room and he was moaning. I heard a nurse say she would rather die than have a BMT. It must be the worst thing in the world.

April 10

Chemo, chemo, chemo. Angela picked out her wedding gown.

April 28

Last night I woke up in the middle of the night. Mom was asleep in the chair but I didn't want to wake her because if I told her how scared I felt I knew it would scare her worse and then I would have to tell her everything was fine so she'd stop being scared but everything <u>is</u> <u>not</u> fine. I called for the Z'bras in my mind over and over but nothing happened. Maybe it's because I was the kind of friend who only wanted to be with them when I was sick. It took me a long time to fall back asleep. I hate the night. It is full of monsters.

CHAPTER NINETEEN

The Ache

May 15

TEN THINGS THAT MAKE ME MAD!!!
1. I am <u>still</u> in the hospital.
2. I am a fat and bald cancer kid again.
3. I have an indwelling catheter now.
4. No school and no talent contest.
5. Darlene was mean but she got well.
6. I am nice but I keep getting sicker.
7. The Z'bras deserted me and

_____

"Well, well, writing in your journal, I see," Dr. Franklin observed jovially as he and Angela strode into Becky's room, both of her parents behind them. Becky was surprised to see her dad. Who was home with Lee?

She closed the journal and put it under her pillow.

"So, Becky, let's chat about the next phase of your treatment," Dr. Franklin said in that too-hearty voice Becky hated. It was his bad news voice.

Becky folded her arms and waited. Her parents came to her bedside.

"It's quite a challenge to keep you in remission, young lady," he went on.

Her mother looked at her father, both their faces happy masks pulled too tight. Then her father reached for her mother's hand. He squeezed it.

She knew.

"You want me to have a bone marrow transplant," Becky said flatly.

"It's not common for ALL, but we think it's your best option," Dr. Franklin said. "A bone marrow transplant is—"

"I know what it is."

Her mother ran one hand over Becky's forehead as if there were still hair to smooth back. "It'll make you sick for a little while, honey, but then you'll be all better and finally all of this will be over."

"And then do I get to live happily ever after, dear?" Becky asked in her best tough-girl Darlene voice.

"We know it's scary, Becks," her father said.

She shrugged, then turned to the wall. "I'd like to be alone now, *Maman* and *Papa*." She pronounced their names the French way, like Darlene had. "Ta-ta."

"We're here whenever you need us, Becks," she heard her dad say. Then everyone left her room.

Good. God bless, good-bye, have a swell life.

"I'm still here, Becks," her mother said quietly.

"And me," Angela added.

Correction. Not everyone.

"Do you want to talk about it?" her mom asked.

Silence.

"Okay then, I'll talk," her mother said.

Becky could tell her mom was trying very hard to sound strong. But that only made Becky madder.

"Dad and I and Lee were typed to see if one of us is a good donor match for you," her mom went on.

"Nice of you to tell me about it." Becky sneered.

"Lee is a match. Which means there's a good chance that the transplant will work."

"Tell that to some rookie," Becky snapped.

"Becks?" She felt her mom's soft touch on her back. "Would you rather talk to Daddy? Or to Dr. Franklin?"

"No."

"Let's try this later, then, sweetie," her mom said. Becky heard her whisper something to Angela and then leave the room.

She rolled over and glowered at the nurse.

"I know you want me to go too," Angela said. "Your mom said we can talk about the BMT if you want. So you choose. Me or someone else. Now or later."

"You. Now," Becky said tersely. "Get it over with."

Angela sat on the end of Becky's bed. "Okay. First, you'll have much stronger chemo to kill off as many cancer cells as possible, then—"

"TBR," Becky filled in. "And I can look forward to lots and lots of lovely mouth sores. La-de-da."

Angela nodded. "You might have trouble breathing—"

"*Breathing?*" Becky broke in. No one had ever said anything to her about having trouble breathing.

"Only because your mouth and throat may be very sore. But we can give you oxygen through a—"

"You die if you don't breathe!"

"You won't die, Becky." Angela reached for one of Becky's hands, but Becky pulled it away.

"How do you know?"

The nurse sat there, mute.

"You *don't* know, do you?" Becky accused. "Not for sure."

"Do you want to talk about it?"

Fear squeezed Becky's heart. "No! Stop asking me that. Go away and leave me alone!"

The nurse hesitated a moment; then she left too.

Becky held her stuffed zebra to her chest, shut her eyes, and rocked back and forth. "I'm not going to die," she chanted. "I'm not going to die, I'm not going to die."

"Excellent positive thinking," a familiar voice said.

She opened her eyes. Ice Z.

There he was, at the door. Zip and Zap too, all three the size of Cape mountain zebra foals.

"Are you really here?" Becky asked hopefully. "I'm not dreaming this?"

"Really and truly," Zip said as they gathered around her bed.

"And we missed you so much," Zap chimed in.

"But I called for you all the time," Becky said, angry again. "And you didn't come."

"We know," Zap said.

"If you missed me so much, why didn't you come?"

"As Papa Zeke would say," Ice Z began, "the answer to your question is . . . I don't know."

"No one knows anything and I'm sick of it."

"It's like this," Ice Z said. "We know everything about you. But we don't know everything about everything."

"What do you mean?" Becky asked crossly.

"Well," Zip began, "we heard Angela talking about the bone marrow transplant—we were outside your door. But we already knew."

"I hate her," Becky said viciously. "And I hate Dr. Franklin. And I hate my parents. Especially my mother. She lied to me from the first day I got here. She said the bone marrow aspiration would only hurt a *little*. My hair might get a *little* thinner. My throat might get a *little* sore. I'd only be sick for a *little* while. Well, it's not 'a little.' *Nothing* is 'a little'!"

"We know," the Z'bras said.

"I hate everyone!"

"We understand," Ice Z said.

Becky clenched her fists. "No, you don't, so don't say you do. *You* don't have cancer. *You* don't have to go through this. *You* only come around when you feel like it. I hate the three of you most of all. Get out of here."

The Z'bras looked at each other uncertainly.

"You heard me," Becky yelled. "Go away and leave me alone!" She threw her toy zebra at Ice Z with all her might. It fell to the floor. Alone, abandoned, afraid.

Sadly, heads low, the Z'bras walked to the door, Ice Z stepping carefully over the tattered zebra.

From outside her window, Becky thought she heard the chilling roar of a distant lion. But that was impossible, wasn't it?

"Wait," Becky called to the Z'bras. They stopped.

"If you really know everything about me," Becky said, her voice defiant, "you know if I'm going to die. I want you to tell me the truth."

Ice Z picked up the toy zebra in his mouth, brought it to Becky, and dropped it gently into her lap. "Predators can be beaten, you know."

"We outran those lions," Zip reminded her.

"That's true," Becky said. "They didn't get you."

"The predators don't always win," Ice Z said.

Zap nodded. "You've got to fight to the finish."

Becky squeezed her zebra tightly. "But how can I? Papa Zeke was right. I'm not really a very plucky person at all," she said softly.

"It takes a very plucky person," Zip and Zap said, "to admit that she isn't very plucky."

Ice Z raised one hoof in salute. "You have serious courage, Becks."

"I don't have serious courage." The ache of welled-up tears began behind her eyes. "The truth is . . . The truth is . . . I'm scared all the time."

At last, she had said it. The ache swelled until there was no room left inside for the tears that finally rained down her cheeks, as her heart shattered into a million pieces. "I'm scared," she sobbed. "I'm so scared."

For a long time they let her cry. Ice Z nuzzled her cheek gently and let the tears fall on his black nose.

"Becks," he said finally, "being scared doesn't mean you don't have courage."

"It doesn't?" Becky sobbed.

"Not at all," Ice Z insisted. "True courage is admitting you're scared and fighting on anyway." He offered her one of his soft ears, and she wiped her eyes.

"Could you three stay with me?" Becky asked. "If I fall asleep, can you be here when I wake up?"

"We'll be here," the Z'bras promised. The mares lifted her blanket with their teeth, gently covering her, then tucked her in with their noses. Becky smiled, her lips still trembling, her eyes red-rimmed.

"I'm sorry I said what I said before. I don't hate you."

The Z'bras replied with one loving voice.

"We know."

CHAPTER TWENTY
The Decision

May 20

TEN THINGS THAT MAKE ME HAPPY!!!
1. I have been off chemo for three days to give me a rest before TBR and I feel _so_ _much_ better.
2. Lee is excited about being my donor.
3. Mrs. Hudson visits me every week.
4. The Z'bras are at the hospital all the time and

———————————————

"Quit it!" Becky giggled, pushing Zap's nose away. "I want to finish this."

"Write later." Zap picked up an apple from Becky's

tray, flipped it in the air, and caught it perfectly on her own nose.

"Excellent!" Becky exclaimed. Zap flipped the apple back to her. "Hey, I thought of a good one for you to tell Papa Zeke. If he steps on Shlep's toes by mistake, he should tell Shlep, 'Well, who told you to go around barefoot?' "

The Z'bras laughed, and Becky laughed with them.

"What's so funny?" came a voice from Becky's doorway. It was Ashley Chaffin.

With Sara Bowder.

"Nothing," Becky said, sliding her journal under the sheets. She felt very self-conscious. Her head was bald again, and the baseball cap she usually wore now hung on the bedpost.

"Can we come in?" Sara asked hesitantly as the Z'bras moved to the far corner of the room.

"Have a seat," Becky said, grabbing the cap and slamming it on her head. Sara took a seat by the bed while Ashley gingerly made her way to the other chair, her arms pressed to her sides as if the room were contaminated.

Becky's eyes slid over to Sara, who had come to visit her before and had sworn she wasn't friends with Ashley anymore.

"Um," Sara mumbled, unable to look at Becky.

"Mrs. Hudson said we should come see you before your bone marrow thingie."

"Bone marrow *transplant*," Ashley corrected. "It was on our last health test. I got an A."

"She's obnoxious!" Zip and Zap exclaimed.

Becky gave Sara a cold look. "So, you and Ashley. Together."

Sara's face reddened. "Well, she asked if I was coming because her mom couldn't drive her, and I said—"

"Oh, just tell the truth, Sara," Ashley said, tossing her hair over her shoulder. "You do whatever I tell you to, and you tell me whatever I want to know."

Sara looked at the floor. "I do not."

"You don't?" Ashley challenged. "Then how do I know that Becky's secret dream is to become a famous singer and that she practices by singing into her hairbrush?"

"Sara, you *told* her?" Becky couldn't believe it.

Sara hung her head. "I'm sorry," she whispered.

"Ashley is the meanest human ever," Zap decided.

"She's also the most popular girl in our class," Becky told the Z'bras, so upset that she didn't care if the girls overheard her.

Ashley whirled around to look in the corner. Nothing was there. "Becky, who are you talking to?"

"Some predators take down the weak ones with words," Ice Z said, glaring at Ashley.

"I know," Becky agreed.

"Becky?" Ashley repeated, her voice louder now. *"Who are you talking to?"*

"No one."

Ashley shrugged, then smiled. "The end-of-the-year talent contest is Friday," she said, her voice oozing sweetness. "Everyone's upset that you can't be in it. Especially me."

"Liar, liar, pants on fire," Zip and Zap sang.

"Machoni rafiki, moyoni mnafiki," Becky commented.

"What?" Ashley asked.

"Ha!" Zap barked. "Good one, Becks!"

Becky smiled. "Thank you."

"Thank you for what?" Ashley demanded.

"Hey, Becky," Ice Z began, "maybe you *could* compete."

Becky shook her head. "I can't."

"Can't what?" Sara asked.

"Nothing," Becky muttered.

Ashley looked at the corner again. "But you keep talking to someone over there!"

"Come on, Becks," Ice Z cajoled. "You don't start radiation until Saturday. After that you might not even be able to talk for a while. This could be your last chance."

"I *can't*," Becky insisted.

"You can!" Zap said. "You can, you can, you—"

"I can't, and quit pushing me! My parents say—"

"It's not their life, Becky," Ice Z said. "It's yours. What do *you* say?"

"Ick, the cancer must be in her brain," Ashley hissed to Sara, pointing a finger at her right temple and making a tight circle.

"What do you say, Becky?" Ice Z repeated.

Ashley stood up and moved cautiously toward the door. "Well, bye. So long. We're leaving now."

"Becky—," the Z'bras began.

"Let's go, Sara," Ashley ordered.

"—you have—"

"Sara, I *said* let's go."

"—true courage." The Z'bras voices rang out.

"I'm sorry," Sara mouthed as she followed Ashley out the door. Then Ashley stuck her head back inside.

"Oh, Becky? I'll come show you my ribbon after I win," she said smugly.

True courage. Did she?

Becky took a deep breath, her heart pounding. "Wait, Ashley. I'm . . . I'm going to be in the talent contest."

Ashley laughed derisively as Sara joined her in the doorway. "You can't be in it. You're too sick."

"I can too be in it," Becky insisted. "I might even win that ribbon myself, Ashley Chaffin."

"Well, how snotty can you get?" Ashley snapped. "We only came to visit you because Hudson's giving extra credit for it. Come on, Sara." She disappeared, but Sara came back to Becky's bed.

"That's not why I came," she said.

"How can you be friends with her?" Becky asked.

Sara looped her hair behind her ears. "You know how she can be. When I stopped doing everything she told me to do, she made my life miserable. I couldn't stand it. I'm really sorry, Becky."

"I'm sorry too," Becky said. "Not for me. For you."

"Sara, let's go!" Ashley's voice echoed in the corridor. Sara fled, closing the door behind her.

Becky turned to the Z'bras. "She used to be my best friend. But she's weak."

The Z'bras nodded.

"Maybe she'll change," Becky said. "It's possible." A slow smile spread across her face. "I stood up to Ashley Chaffin. Did you see the look on her face when I told her I'm competing in the talent contest?"

"You were plucky," Ice Z said.

Becky's smile grew even bigger. "I was, wasn't I? Now all I have to do is to tell—"

A knock at the door. Her parents.

"—my parents," Becky squeaked as they entered.

Her father laughed. "Yep, last time I checked, we're still your parents." He kissed her cheek. "How's my beautiful daughter feeling?"

"Fine," Becky said automatically.

"Wro-ong!" Zip and Zap sang.

"Well, not altogether fine," she amended nervously. "That is . . . I have something to tell both of you."

Her mother fluffed her pillow. "We're listening."

Becky licked her lips. This was really, really hard.

You've done harder things, Becky, said a voice in her head. *You can do this.*

Papa Zeke! She hadn't heard his voice in such a long time, and she missed him so much. It gave her courage.

"Mom, Dad, I've made a decision," she said firmly. "I'm going to be in the talent contest on Friday."

"Out of the question," her mother replied.

"But I want to while I still can."

Her mother got very busy fixing her blanket. "Once you get all better you can—"

"But what if I don't *get* better?"

"Of course you're getting better," Mrs. Zaslow said sharply. "You're going to feel a little worse from the transplant for a little while, but then—"

"Mom." Becky reached for her mother's hand. "The truth is, no one knows for sure if I'm ever going to get better. And I don't want to put off living because I might be . . ."

Becky saw the misery etched on her mother's face, misery she was causing.

"Because I might be . . ."

No. She couldn't say it.

True courage. You can do this.

"Dying."

Her mother stood frozen, like a trapped zebra surrounded by ravenous lions.

Becky forced herself to go on. "I want to be in the talent contest. And unless Dr. Franklin says I can't, I think it should be my decision. Because it's my life."

Mr. Zaslow put his arms around Mrs. Zaslow as the Z'bras trotted over to Becky and nuzzled against her.

"I think that's fine, Becks," her father told her, holding his wife close. "It's just fine."

CHAPTER TWENTY-ONE

The Blue Ribbon

May 23

The talent contest is tonight. Dr. Franklin is letting me leave the hospital for three hours to be in it. I am very scared. Yesterday I started to feel really sick. I start TBR tomorrow and I will feel even sicker. I am so tired I can hardly get out of bed. What if I can't do it? I tell myself that the only failure is not to try. The Z'bras promise to be with me no matter what. They say I have true courage. But what if they are wrong?

———————————

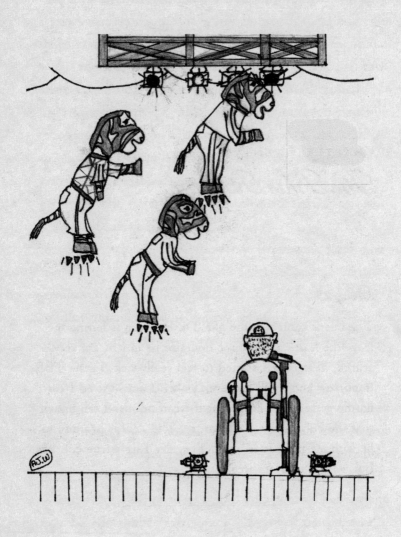

There were two rows of chairs at the rear of the stage, where Becky sat with all the other performers. Her parents and Lee sat behind her, even though everyone else's family sat out in the audience. She had asked hers to sit with her, and she didn't care what anyone thought.

Channa Gold finished her tumbling routine and the audience applauded. Sara and Micah, who were working as crew, ran to pull the gymnastics mat off the stage.

As they worked, Becky could feel everyone staring at her. She knew she looked strange, despite her pretty new dress. Her face was fat from chemo and she wore a baseball cap on her bald head. It seemed like such a long time since she had been like everyone else, just another sixth-grader.

She glanced out at the audience and up to the balcony. The Z'bras were sitting on the balcony railing, and when Becky caught their eye, they each happily waved a hoof at her.

"Becky?" It was Mrs. Hudson, who was the announcer for the talent contest. She wore a festive *kanga* from her native Tanzania for the occasion. "I'm glad you're here. You are very, very brave."

"Thank you," Becky said softly. It took so much energy just to talk. She didn't want to have to be brave.

Lee leaned forward. "Hey, Mrs. Hudson, did you know I'm gonna be Becky's bone marrow donor?"

Mrs. Hudson nodded. "You are also very brave."

He shrugged. "I know."

The stage now clear, Mrs. Hudson went to the microphone and introduced Ashley, who ran out onstage. As her music came up, she lip-synched to "Yankee Doodle Dandy." Her Uncle Sam top hat matched her sequined tuxedo jacket, and even from behind, Becky could see that her choreography was dazzling.

"Hey, that girl is cheating," Lee whispered loudly. "She isn't even the one singing!"

"It's called lip-synching," Mrs. Zaslow explained.

"Lip *stinking*," Lee said. "Becky's gonna smush her."

"Shhh," Becky told him, but she grinned.

Ashley finished by landing in a split and flinging her arms overhead. The audience applauded loudly as she bowed. Becky applauded too but saw up in the balcony that the Z'bras were sitting with their hooves crossed.

Sara slid into the seat next to Becky. "Hi," she said.

Becky didn't say anything.

"I don't blame you for being mad at me, Becky," Sara told her as Ashley turned and walked regally toward them. "I just wanted to say that—"

"Excuse me," Ashley interrupted, panting a little from her routine. "Sara, you're in my seat."

Sara jumped up, and Ashley sat down, flashing Becky

a smug look of triumph. Becky looked away, and Ashley turned back to Sara.

"So, I was really good, wasn't I?" Ashley asked.

"No," Lee mumbled.

Sara looked at Becky and then back at Ashley. "Oh, yeah, you were great, Ashley," she agreed, loudly enough for everyone to hear. "Except for that icky green thing hanging out of your nose." Ashley sprang to her feet to check for an icky green thing, and all the kids onstage burst out laughing.

Mrs. Hudson came to Becky and sat next to her, taking Becky's chilly hands in her own. "Are you ready?"

Becky nodded.

"*Kila jambo na wakati wake,* Becky. 'There is a time for everything,' " the teacher translated. "And this is your time to shine." She went to the microphone and waited for the audience to quiet.

"We have one final act in our contest, after which all the students in grade six will vote for the winner," Mrs. Hudson said. "Singing her favorite song, 'The Lion Sleeps Tonight,' I am honored to introduce Becky Zaslow."

Becky stood. The crowd cheered as if she were some famous celebrity. But she felt so weak. And the microphone looked so far away. She took a few steps toward it, faltered, and glanced unsteadily back at her mother, who instantly moved to help her. Her father put his hand lightly on her mother's arm, and her mother sat down again.

Becky would have to do this by herself.

It seemed to take forever to reach the microphone, but she did it. The Z'bras, who had dashed down from the balcony, stood behind her on the stage as backup singers, invisible to everyone but Becky.

The auditorium quieted. Becky breathed heavily, winded from walking to the microphone.

" 'Wimoweh, a-wimoweh, a-wimoweh, a-wimoweh,' " the Z'bras began in their best three-part harmony, bobbing their striped heads together to the beat.

This was where Becky was supposed to come in. She opened her mouth. The smallest of voices came out.

In the jungle, the mighty . . . the mighty . . .

She gasped, unable to get enough air to sing.

"Try again," Ice Z urged. "You can do it!"

Becky put her mouth right up to the microphone. The amplified sound of her heavy breathing echoed through the hushed auditorium. She filled her lungs as best she could.

In the jungle, the mighty . . . mighty . . .

She stopped. The silence felt like a weight, choking her. Everyone stared. No one moved.

Becky put her mouth to the microphone again. "I thought I could do it," she whispered, "but I can't. I'm too tired to sing."

She turned, and her frightened eyes met her father's. He jumped up to help her. Part of her wanted to fly into his arms and let him make everything all right. But he couldn't. She knew that. And this time it was her mother who put her hand on her husband's arm. He stopped, and part of Becky was very sad. But the part of her that knew she had to do this herself was glad.

She still had the Z'bras. She turned to them.

They were gone.

But they had promised to stay with her.

So they were liars too.

She was all alone.

Never. She heard Papa Zeke's voice. *Look up.*

She did. There, floating overhead like three minia-ture balloons in the Thanksgiving Day parade, were the Z'bras.

"Sorry, wanted a better view," Zap explained.

"From up here—" Zip began.

"—you look beautiful," Ice Z finished.

Mrs. Hudson hurried to Becky and put her arm around her. "It's all right, Becky. You tried your best and that is what's most important. Now, if everyone in grade six will please write down their choice for winner, the ushers will collect your votes and turn them in."

"Becky?"

It was her dad, with the wheelchair they'd left backstage. Her parents helped Becky into it and wheeled her offstage where the other student performers were congregated, marking their ballots.

Ashley and Sara stood near Becky. Becky could hear every word they said as she marked her own ballot.

"You're voting for me, aren't you?" Ashley asked Sara.

"No," Sara said, moving away from Ashley and coming over to Becky. "No one is voting for you. Everyone is voting for Becky."

Becky saw Ashley scan the faces of the students around her as they all nodded their agreement with Sara. No one was voting for Ashley. Everyone really *was* voting for her.

For the very first time that Becky could remember, Ashley Chaffin stood alone.

A flicker of rage crossed Ashley's face. Then she smiled knowingly and ran onto the stage.

"Mrs. Hudson, Mrs. Hudson!" she called. "I don't think we even need to count the ballots." She snatched the microphone from the startled teacher and gave the audience her perkiest smile. "The entire sixth grade agrees. The winner of the talent contest is . . . Becky Zaslow!"

The audience leaped to its feet, applauding wildly, roaring with approval. Lee insisted on being the one to push Becky in her wheelchair out to center stage. Becky stood up uncertainly and Mrs. Hudson put an arm around her.

"Congratulations, Becky!" the teacher said. "You won."

She handed Becky the shiny blue ribbon that Becky had dreamed about for so long. Her picture would forever be in the display case outside the principal's office, with the pictures of all the past winners. She had won. The blue ribbon in her hands proved it.

Everyone was standing, cheering for her, Rebecca Rose Zaslow.

The worst experiences can offer the best lessons, Becky. But not if you forget to remember.

Becky looked at the blue ribbon, then up at her teacher. "I didn't win, Mrs. Hudson."

"But—"

"Trying your best is important. But this is a talent *contest*. I wasn't the best. I only won because you all feel sorry for me. I never wanted you to feel sorry for me. I just wanted to be treated like everyone else. I don't want to win unless I deserve it."

Panting from the exertion of talking, Becky paused and caught her breath. Then she held the ribbon out to Ashley. "Congratulations, Ashley," she said. "You won."

Slowly Ashley walked over to Becky. Becky handed her the blue ribbon. Their eyes met.

But this time it was Ashley who broke first.

That was when Becky turned to her family.

"I'm ready to go back to the hospital now," she said.

CHAPTER TWENTY-TWO

The Crossing

"MAY TWENTY-SEVENTH," Becky said weakly into the cassette recorder. She thought for a moment before continuing.

What's funny is how I was worried about mouth sores and not being able to talk, but I don't have sores yet and I can talk fine. Also I can breathe fine so far and don't need oxygen. I was scared about that. But I am very, very tired and a lot of places on me hurt. Also sometimes my hands shake too much for me to write. My parents got me this little recorder so I can keep up my journal. When I'm better I will write all this down. I bet that will take a really long

time! They just finished infusing me with Lee's bone marrow. He told everyone that it didn't hurt when they stuck the needle into his hipbone. The part he didn't tell is that they put him to sleep before they did it.

"Tell about the radiation room," Zip said. She floated languidly five feet above Becky's head, with Zap and Ice Z.

Becky leaned back. Her head hurt. "*One* of us can't float," she reminded Zip. "Let me try to get comfortable."

"I have an idea," Zap said. "Lift your head." She floated down softly onto Becky's bed. "There. I'll be your pillow."

Becky leaned back and nestled her head against Zap's belly. "Oh, that's much better," she sighed. She spoke into her recorder again.

For three days I had TBR in a special room with two big cobalt radiation machines. Radiation makes you really sick. My face got all red and my neck swelled up like when I had the mumps and it made me throw up over and over. I didn't want to ask for help because I knew the machine would be turned off and the TBR would take longer. Everyone thought I was in there alone but the Z'bras were with me the whole time. Ice Z told the story of Zink the zebra again. It's my favorite, except Zink should live happily ever after at the end.

Now I am in the same BMT isolation room Joe used to be in. There is a special air filter system in here to prevent germs. I can't have visitors so I won't get germs, and even Dr. Franklin and the nurses wear masks when they come in. Let's see, what else . . .

"This thing is quite the fashion risk." Angela's voice was muffled by her mask as she came in to check on Becky. "The least they could do is offer a choice of colors, huh?"

"We don't have to wear 'em!" the Z'bras singsonged as Zap floated back up to the ceiling.

Angela checked Becky's pulse, then wrote something on her chart. "I hope you're putting in your journal how incredibly cute I am."

Becky's shaky hand lifted her recorder to her lips. "And Angela made me say she is incredibly cute," she added.

"Some junior bridesmaid you are," the nurse huffed. "At least turn that thing off before I tell you that I've gained twelve pounds since I bought my wedding gown. If I don't lose it, I'll be going down the aisle in my birthday suit."

"Some of my best friends look very nice in their birthday suits," Becky said, looking up at the Z'bras.

"Do-wahhh!" the Z'bras sang happily.

Suddenly Becky shivered. She put down her recorder and burrowed farther under her blankets. She felt very cold. Angela frowned, put a thermometer under Becky's tongue, then took it out and read it.

"I just spiked a fever, huh?" Becky whispered.

"A touch," Angela said, so lightly that Becky knew it was more than a touch. "I'll ask Dr. Franklin to look in on you." She added another blanket to Becky's bed and left.

Immediately the Z'bras floated down to her.

"All of a sudden I feel awful," Becky told them anxiously. "I'm freezing."

"It's the radiation," Ice Z reminded her. "This is the hardest part. But remember, Becky, you have true courage."

She couldn't stop shivering. "How come true courage is something you have to prove over and over? And how come we couldn't go to the Serengeti when I was in the TBR room, even though I wanted to so much?"

"As Papa Zeke would say," Zap began, "the answer to your question is . . ."

"I don't know," Becky whispered, and closed her eyes. "I miss Papa Zeke. And the herd. How's Shlep?"

Maybe this is a good time for you to come and find out for yourself.

Becky's eyes popped open. "Did you hear that?"

"Think Zink," the Z'bras told her. "Think Zink."

Becky shut her eyes again and concentrated on the Zink story with all her might. And just as Dr. Franklin came into her room, his face half hidden behind his mask but his eyes hyperalert, she was gone.

LUB-DUB. A beat of her heart. Becky flew free in the tunnel of shimmering colors and beautiful music. Before the next lub-dub of her heart, she landed in Africa.

She expected to open her eyes to a bright blue sky, green savanna grass, and Papa Zeke and the herd waiting to greet her. Instead, she found herself on the bank of a swollen river amid thousands of bellowing, *kwa*'ing zebras. They flung themselves into the furiously churning water, madly paddling to the other side.

Some were trampled on the riverbank. Others, weak or just unlucky, screamed pitifully as they were swept downstream to the hungry crocodiles.

The noise was horrific.

"It's too terrible, make it stop!" Becky screamed.

No zebra paid attention to her.

She felt mud ooze into her sneakers. She was fully

dressed. She touched her head. She had hair! She felt healthy, strong, perfectly normal, but—

"Help!" a high-pitched voice screeched over the din. "Ice Z! Come back for me!"

Shlep! Becky whirled around. She was sure she'd heard him. But all she saw were more frightened zebras, hundreds and thousands of them, splashing into the rushing river.

"He-e-elp!" she heard again.

There he was! Fifty yards down the riverbank, a small, furry, green thing standing alone.

"Shlep!" Dodging zebras, she ran to him through the mud.

"Becky!" He jumped up and down with joy, then took a flying leap into her arms. "I lost the herd!"

"You mean they're across?"

Shlep nodded. He wrapped his legs around her waist and his arms around her neck. "It was awful. I made a vow to be a real zebra and swim this time. I made Ice Z go without me. I was gonna do it. I was. But then I saw this foal get crushed, and then a crocodile ate her, and—"

"And you lost your courage," Becky concluded sympathetically, patting his back.

He nodded, burying his head in her neck.

"They'll come back for you, Shlep," she assured him.

"No," the monkey lamented. "I failed my zebra test.

They're gone. Now I'll be all alone forever. Alone is the worst thing you can be. Unless you can stay with me?"

He turned his face hopefully to her.

"I belong somewhere else, Shlep," she said gently.

"I understand. It's okay." The monkey climbed down and gave her leg one last hug. "I'll never forget you, Becky. Never." Slowly, head hanging, he walked away.

Becky watched him. Shlep was right. Alone was the worst thing you could be.

"Shlep, wait!" Becky called and ran to him. "Look, I'm a good swimmer. Do you think you could stay on my back?"

Shlep's eyes lit up. "You'd swim the Mara? For me?"

Becky nodded.

"It's really, really, really hard, Becky." Shlep hopped anxiously from one foot to the other. "A big zebra can squish you or kick you in the head by mistake. Or the current can push you downstream, where those mean crocodiles with those big, pointy teeth are waiting to eat you, and—"

"Shlep?" Becky interrupted.

"Huh?"

"I know."

"Oh."

Becky motioned to him, and he scrambled onto her

180

back and wrapped his arms around her neck. She edged carefully toward the riverbank.

"Are you scared?" Shlep asked her.

"Very," Becky admitted.

"Uh-oh," Shlep squeaked.

"No, it's okay," Becky told him. "Are you ready?"

Shlep nodded.

She took three tentative steps into the water and found herself up to her waist. Before she could begin to swim, the ferocious current knocked her off her feet, pushing her downstream. She refused to give in, kicking her legs powerfully and pulling her arms as Shlep clung to her back.

Her right arm cut through the water, then her left. Right, left, right, left, using every ounce of her strength. They were halfway across now. Shlep's claws dug into her neck and he screeched hysterical monkey noises in her ear. Panicky zebras bellowed all around them.

Becky's arms ached with exhaustion, her chest pounded, she sucked air through burning lungs, but she wouldn't give up. Right, left, right, left. She could see the other side now. She had to keep going. Had to.

The current quickened. Becky felt herself weakening, losing to the relentless pull, until all she could do was dog-paddle frantically and try to keep them afloat.

"Fight," she ordered herself. "Fight harder." She forced her legs to keep kicking. *I. Will. Not. Give. Up.*

Her right leg brushed something. A boulder? A tree stump? If only she could find it again, so she could push off it. She thrashed her legs. It had to be there, somewhere, it had to be. If only—

She hit it again! This time she pushed off it as hard as she could. It was the extra boost she needed, and she propelled her arms with a strength she had never known she possessed.

Finally both her hands touched the muddy river bottom. With one last groan of exertion, she heaved herself ashore and fell over panting as Shlep covered her face with wet monkey kisses.

"You did it! You did it!" he cried. "You're my hero!"

For many moments she lay there, too worn out to speak. Finally she sat up. To the west, thousands of zebras had gathered back into their herds, black and white as far as the eye could see. To the east, hundreds more zebras had done the same.

All the herds looked alike.

"Becky?" Shlep asked uncertainly.

She stood up and took his paw. Calmly, for a long, long time, her eyes swept over the zebras.

"Becky?" Shlep asked again, panic in his voice.

"Patience is a virtue, Shlep," she told him. She

focused on one herd, then the next, then the next, the next, the next, the next, the next . . .

There! Ice Z's herd. Five hundred yards to the right.

Hand in paw, Becky and Shlep ran toward it. Ice Z saw them coming, *kwa*'d joyfully, and led the herd in a gallop to them. The Z'bras nuzzled happily against Becky, while the others danced and pranced in welcome.

Zuzi touched Becky's arm with her snout. "Papa Zeke didn't tell us you were coming. We've missed you so much!"

"Did you swim the Mara, Shlep?" Zip asked.

Shlep puffed out his scrawny chest. "Kinda-sorta." His gaze slid over to Becky. He was a terrible liar. "Kinda-sorta on Becky's back," he admitted guiltily.

Zilch strode over to the monkey. "Oh, it's you," he uttered disdainfully. "How unfortunate. I was certain I had seen a croc with green fur in his teeth."

"Watch the mean remarks, mister."

The herd parted to let Papa Zeke through. He gave Becky a grin more gummy than toothy. "So. Here you are."

Becky nodded.

"You swam the Mara. With the Shlepper on your back, yet. It's not so easy."

She nodded again.

"And then you found us in the midst of all these

zebras," Papa Zeke went on. "How did you recognize us?"

Becky smiled. "I didn't think I could. But then I remembered how no two zebras have the same stripes. So it wasn't any harder than being in a big crowd of people and trying to find my own family."

"We're your family too, Becks," Ice Z said.

"Forever and ever," the herd chorused.

"Exactly," Papa Zeke said. He beckoned to Becky with a now arthritic foreleg.

She went to him. "Yes, Papa Zeke?"

"Becky," he said. There was pride in his gruff old voice. "You were plucky."

CHAPTER TWENTY-THREE
The Visitor

BECKY WHISPERED into her cassette recorder.

_____

June 14

My BMT was two weeks ago. Things are not going too
well. I have bad sores in my mouth and throat. And I have
graft-versus-host disease, which means the new marrow is
making me sick instead of well. I have an itchy GVHD
rash but lots of people get it, it doesn't have to mean
you're in trouble. Joe had bad GVHD but he got better
and finally went home. Um, I have a respiratory infection
but it doesn't hurt. I sleep a lot. Mom and Dad are
allowed in my room now even though it's against the rules.

_____

"Don't tire yourself out, Becks," Mr. Zaslow warned from behind his mask. He had a law enforcement magazine on his lap, but he wasn't reading it.

"I won't." Becky looked up at the Z'bras, who floated on their backs near the ceiling, hooves crossed behind their heads as if they were sunbathing at the beach.

I feel bad that he worries so much, Becky told them silently. They could hear each other's thoughts now, so they didn't have to speak.

That's what parents do, Ice Z said.

It still makes me feel bad. How come you can hear my thoughts, but they can't? And don't say you don't know.

We don't know.

Becky sighed. *That doesn't make any sense. Do you ever wonder why so many things don't make sense, Z'bras?*

I sure do, Zap said. She floated her head downward, so her tail was against the ceiling. *Like, for example, when it's perfectly warm outside, why do humans wear clothes?*

Becky laughed. "That's not exactly what I meant."

"What?" her father asked, alarmed.

Oops. I said it aloud!

Oops, the two mares agreed.

"Nothing, Dad," Becky told him. "I was just thinking."

Her father's cellular phone rang. He took it out of his pocket. "Hello? . . . Hey, Lee, what's up? . . . No, not yet . . . I will . . . I promise . . . Lee, put your mom—

"Your brother just hung up on me," her father said, putting the phone away. "He's mad because I didn't give you the present he made for you yet." Mr. Zaslow rummaged through the bag of stuff he'd brought with him.

"Ah, here it is."

He handed Becky a large blue ribbon made from construction paper. In Lee's messy printing it read:

BEKCY IS #1. YU DU NOT LIP-STINK.

"It was his own idea," her father went on. "He wouldn't let us help."

"I love it," Becky said.

Her father put the ribbon on the nightstand. "He's such a great kid. And smart. But he doesn't try in reading at all."

"I was like that with math, remember?" Becky asked. "I was scared I couldn't do it, so I wouldn't try. But once I found out I *could* do it, I was fine."

"Lee can do math, but he's scared he doesn't read well, so it's hard to get him to read at all." Her father smiled down at her. "How did I get two such great kids who are so hard on themselves, Becks?"

"I'll tell him how much I love the ribbon," Becky promised. She suddenly felt very tired. "I think I'll take a nap now, okay?"

"Sure, sweetie." He tucked the blanket around her and pressed his masked mouth to her forehead. "Good night, sleep tight, don't let the bedbugs bite."

Gee, our mom used to say the same thing, Zap marveled. *Only instead of bedbugs, she said "don't let the sweat bees sting."*

That's funny. Becky closed her eyes and tried to get comfortable. Her chest felt funny. *Z'bras? I think it's getting harder to breathe.*

Tell your dad, Ice Z said.

I don't want to scare him.

He'll be more scared if you don't tell him.

I know you're right. But I'll just wait a little while and see if it gets better.

Becky heard someone come in and she opened her eyes. It was Angela. She'd drawn a mustache and a big grinning mouth with missing teeth on her surgical mask.

"Wear that to your wedding," Becky panted. "I dare you."

"Oh, sure, sabotage my future," Angela groused. She frowned at Becky. "What's with the breathing?"

Instantly Mr. Zaslow was up out of his chair. "What about her breathing?"

"Nothing," Becky said quickly, but she was panting even harder.

"I think she overdid it with her tape recorder," Mr. Zaslow said, his voice tense. "That's all it is. Right?"

Angela took Becky's pulse. "I'll be right back." She hurried from the room.

"What is it? What?" Mr. Zaslow asked, following her to the door. He yelled down the hall after her. "Can't I get some answers around here?"

He turned back to his daughter. She was gasping for air like a newly caught fish, her bony chest rising and falling rapidly under the blankets.

"Oh, dear God." Her father's eyes looked huge and helpless. "Hold on, sweetie. It's okay. Just—" He ran out the door after Angela.

Z'bras? I'm scared.

Picture the Serengeti on a perfect day, Ice Z said, his voice deep and calm in her mind. *The sun is shining, everything is peaceful and beautiful. Can you see it?*

I'm too scared to see it.

The whole herd is under the baobab tree, Zap went on. *We're not even fighting. In fact, we're all singing.*

Can you hear it? Zip asked.

I'm too scared to hear it. I can't!

In the jungle, the mighty jungle, the lion sleeps tonight.

The Z'bras sang, slow and sweet.

Angela burst into the room with an oxygen mask and some tubing, Mr. Zaslow right behind her. She plugged the tubing into the wall, turned on a regulator, and placed the mask on Becky's face.

"This is no biggie, Becks," Angela said as she secured the mask. "It's just to help you breathe more easily."

In the jungle, the mighty jungle, the lion sleeps tonight.

"What's she saying?" Becky's father asked frantically. "I can't understand her."

"She's singing," Angela said, lovingly stroking Becky's forehead. "I think she's singing."

June 20

The oxygen mask makes it hard to talk into my tape recorder. Plus, thinking is much easier on my mouth and throat sores than talking. I am getting a drug called morphine now which helps me relax and makes the pain go away but sometimes it makes my mind fuzzy. I don't like that part. But usually it's okay.

Don't forget to say what's good about today, Ice Z reminded her. He lolled in the lounge chair near the window, gigantic pink sunglasses that had been a gift to Becky from Mrs. Hudson balanced on his big, black nose.

What's good about today is how funny you look in those sunglasses.

June 24

Still on oxygen. My respiratory infection is the fungal kind and that is not good, but it doesn't hurt. I sleep a lot. Lee got special permission to come to my room. I wore the blue ribbon he made for me. He looked very scared but I told him a joke and he felt better. I wanted to tell him so many things but I was too tired. Today for the first time I wondered seriously about dying. I don't think Dad could handle it. I will ask the Z'bras about it later. But I have a feeling they will say they don't know.

June 28

I am down but not out!!! Dr. Franklin says my lungs seem better. My mouth sores are better and my GVHD rash is better and sometimes I don't even need my oxygen mask. Mrs. Hudson dropped off some cassette tapes of books for me; that was so nice of her. And here is the best news.

This time my hair is coming in as blond as Ashley Chaffin's! It's kind of thin so far, but I—

———————————

"O Princess of the Sixth Floor," Angela called as she stuck her head in the room. "You have a visitor. If you want her."

Becky took off the oxygen mask. "I thought I wasn't allowed."

"You're not," Angela said. "Too much dieting has worn down my usual steely resolve. However, I can now zip my wedding gown again."

"Who is it?"

"Little Miss Sunshine," Darlene said, stepping into the room around Angela. Her mouth and nose were covered by a mask. She wore a lot of black mascara. Her real hair was brown, short and spiky, the ends dyed bright pink.

"You want her?" Angela asked. Becky nodded.

"Just a few minutes, Darlene," Angela cautioned. "And Becky, don't be afraid to buzz for me." She gave Darlene a warning look before shutting the door behind her.

Darlene peered down at Becky. "You got a Port-A-Cath for meds, huh? And your head went cue ball. Definitely not a rookie anymore. Basically, you look terrible."

"So do you," Becky said, "but at least I have an excuse." She put her oxygen mask back on and inhaled deeply. "If you came to see Joe, he went home."

"I know that." Darlene looked at Becky's hands. "Rash isn't too bad. Your hair's coming back. You don't really look all that totally awful, considering."

"How are you?" Becky asked.

"Hodgkin's-free. But trying to pretend I'm just another normal thirteen-year-old who lives in the burbs and gets hyper over shopping at the mall is excruciating."

"No one could accuse you of being normal," Becky said.

"Ha. And to think you used to be such a mouse."

Darlene leaned against the wall. "At least isolation means no roomie. Which means you won't get stuck with someone as obnoxious as I was."

Becky moved the mask. "I was glad you were my roommate. Even though I thought you hated me."

"Well, I *did* hate you." Darlene shrugged. "You know, I only ever had one other roomie besides you when I was stuck in here. Her name was—"

"Carolyn," Becky filled in. "You mentioned her once."

Darlene raised her eyebrows. "If I'm supposed to be impressed, I'm not." She peeled some nail polish off her pinky. "It's not that Carolyn was so great. But she made me laugh. Which is worth a lot here at Cancer Central."

Becky nodded.

"I was this stupid rookie," Darlene went on, still not looking at Becky. "But Carolyn explained things. Like Magic Mouthwash *before* you get mouth sores. And asking for extra pain meds *before* you need them because it takes so long to actually get them. And a million other things."

Becky nodded again.

"Carolyn had AML," Darlene said, her voice low, "but she was doing really good. We made all these plans. Like we were gonna hitch to Hollywood and become stuntwomen in the movies one day. And the thing is . . . the thing is, she promised me she wouldn't die."

Darlene folded her arms and finally looked at Becky again. "She lied. I *hate* liars. I'll never forgive her for that."

"I'm really sorry," Becky whispered.

"Yeah, yeah." Darlene came back over to Becky's bed, her jaw set hard. "My point is, you shouldn't take it personally that we were never friends. Because caring about anyone in this place is stupid."

"You cared about Joe," Becky said.

"Ah, dear Joe." Darlene posed dramatically. "Yes, I

cared about him deeply, madly, passionately!" She dropped her pose and her voice went back to normal. "That was easy. Because he couldn't have cared less about me."

"Oh."

"Yeah, like you didn't know. Anyway, a word to the not-so-wise. I never cared about you. And you were stupid to care about me."

Becky nodded.

"So. That's all I wanted to say. Good-bye, so long, gotta run—"

"I still do care about you," Becky interrupted.

Darlene clenched her teeth. "Well, don't."

"When I get out of here," Becky began, "we can—"

"Didn't you hear a word I said?" Darlene asked, her voice rising. "Kids die here for no reason. It happens all the time. And you never know who it's going to be. So I really don't want to hear about 'when I get out of here'!"

"Okay, then," Becky whispered.

"Okay." Darlene strutted to the door, then hesitated. "Look, don't make a big thing out of this. . . ."

"Out of what?" Becky asked.

"This. When I said I never cared about you, I lied." Darlene pulled the door open and disappeared.

"I know," Becky said to the empty room. "I know."

CHAPTER TWENTY-FOUR

Two Worlds

MRS. ZASLOW SAT by Becky's bed, a book on her lap, her daughter's right hand in her own. "Mrs. Hudson brought another tape your class made for you right before school ended. You can play it when you wake up. And Lee said that when you get home, you're the only one who is allowed to help him with his reading, not me or Dad. And—"

Mr. Zaslow strode into the room. "I had to call the sitter Lee hates. He had a fit. How's she doing?"

"Better."

He raised his eyebrows but his wife was looking at their daughter. He'd just pulled a chair up next to her when Dr. Franklin tapped on the open door.

"Ah, good, Zaslows, you're both here," he said. "I think we need to discuss treatment options now that—"

"Could we do it later?" Mrs. Zaslow interrupted. "I was about to read Becky a story."

"Mrs. Zaslow, she can't hear you," the doctor said.

"Of course she can." She gave him a brittle smile.

The doctor shook his head. "I'm sorry, but she can't. Now, if and when Becky regains consciousness—"

Mrs. Zaslow jumped out of her chair. "She hears every word you're saying."

"Diane—" her husband began gently.

"*Every word.*" She glared at him.

"I don't know if Becky can hear us or not," he said, going to his wife's side. "But she's getting worse. She's been like this for days, honey."

"I know how painful it is, Mrs. Zaslow," Dr. Franklin said. "We'd hoped for better from the BMT. But you need to hear what I have to say a—"

"No!" Mrs. Zaslow turned on him. "*You* need to hear what *I* have to say, Doctor. I am her mother. And I will never, ever give up on my daughter. Do you hear me? *Do you?*" Her entire body was shaking.

Her husband put his arms around his wife. "Later, Doctor," he said. "We'll talk later."

Dr. Franklin nodded and left.

"Diane, listen to me," Mr. Zaslow said, holding his

wife close. "We have to give Becky a chance to say good-bye. When she wakes up, we have to be hon—"

She broke from his embrace, sat back down next to Becky, and opened the book she'd been reading aloud from earlier. "Now, where were we?" she asked her daughter.

Mr. Zaslow stood by the window, looking out, seeing nothing, as his wife began to read.

"HEY, I know where we can hide," Shlep whispered to Becky. "Up my tree!"

"Sixteen, seventeen . . . ," Zap slowly counted.

Shlep scrambled up the tree; Becky followed. They hid amid the green leaves, trying to smother their laughter.

"Eighteen . . . ," Zap counted. "What's after eighteen?"

"Twem-my!" Zuzi called, her mouth full of star grass.

Zilch groaned.

"Twemmy!" Zap repeated. "Ready or not, here I come." She opened her eyes and started to search, looking all around the tree, near the pond, and in the tall grass, unable to find them.

"She can't find us," Shlep whispered gleefully.

"Zap, I suggest you look up the tree," Zilch told her.

Zap looked up. "I see you, I win!"

"No fair!" Shlep yelped, scrambling down the tree. He ran over to Zilch. "You told."

"Kindly do not breathe on me with that repulsive monkey breath." Zilch waved a hoof in front of Shlep's face.

"That was mean, Zilch," Becky called. She climbed down and went to join Papa Zeke, who was grazing with some other zebras near the pond. The old zebra could barely stand now, his arthritis had gotten so bad.

"Papa Zeke?" Becky asked.

"Yes?"

"Sometimes I think I hear my mom calling me. But I don't want to go back just yet. Is that mean of me?"

The old zebra blinked slowly. "Do you think it's mean?"

Becky thought a moment. "No. Because I *am* going back. But right now I need to be right here."

"Exactly," Papa Zeke agreed.

Becky sat down near the elderly zebra, and Zuzi and Zap wandered over to graze, too. In the distance, Becky could see Ice Z and Zip standing on watch.

"One other thing, Papa Zeke," Becky said as Shlep scampered over and plopped down in her lap. "Whatever happened to the big zebra with the scar?"

"Xerxes? Oh, he left," Zuzi reported blithely.

Shlep shuddered. "All us zebras were really scared that he was gonna fight Ice Z for the herd."

"He didn't?" Becky asked.

Papa Zeke shook his head. "Which only proves, my children, that sometimes the thing you fear the most does not happen."

"But sometimes it does," Becky pointed out.

"Yes." The old zebra nodded. "Sometimes it does."

"Please," Zilch groaned. He'd made his way over to them too. "No more words of wisdom from our fearless, and might I add, *toothless* spiritual leader."

"You are very mean, Zilch," Zap said.

Zuzi nodded. "Everyone hates you."

"Everyone adores me."

"Does not," Zuzi huffed.

"Does too," Zilch insisted.

"Does not."

"Does too."

A huge ruckus erupted as all the zebras took sides, arguing loudly.

"Papa Zeke," Becky implored, "can't you make them stop?"

The old zebra shrugged. "What can I tell you? Zebras aren't perfect."

"Although I come very close." Zilch sniffed.

At that, Shlep dashed back over to Zilch and jumped up and down in his face. "You do not, Zilch! You're the meanest zebra in Africa. In fact, the rest of us zebras don't think you even deserve to be a zebra. Right, you guys?"

Zilch glared at the monkey. "Listen, you pathetic pile of millipede-munching shrunken simian savanna grass. For the last time: You. Are. Not. A. *Zebra!*"

Shlep desperately tried to think of a clever comeback.

"Am too!" he finally said.

"Ha! What you are is a filthy little green *monkey*. And that is what you will always be!" Zilch *kwa*'d furiously and bared his teeth at the small green creature.

Shlep shrank back, then looked around at the others. "Tell him he's wrong, you guys. Tell him I'm a zebra. Go on, tell him."

No zebra spoke.

"Becky?" Shlep asked hopefully. "Papa Zeke?"

The old zebra finished gumming a mouthful of grass. "You are who you are, Shlep. And who you are is wonderful."

Shlep hung his head. "But I'm different."

"Different can be wonderful," Becky told him.

"No," Shlep said, his body sagging. "It isn't. Zilch is right. I'm just a filthy little green . . . *monkey*. There. I said it. I'm not really a zebra at all."

Shlep refused to cry in front of the herd. Instead, he sprinted away, a few tufts of green fur trailing behind him.

"Shlep, wait!" Becky scrambled to her feet, but the monkey kept running.

"Kwa!" Ice Z's alarm ripped through the air. "Kwa-kwa!"

"Predators!" the herd cried, instantly on full alert.

"Everyone, stay with the herd," Ice Z commanded, running over to push Papa Zeke from behind.

"I'll slow you down," Papa Zeke protested.

"We stay together!" Ice Z barked firmly. "Everyone!"

"Run in the middle, Papa Zeke," Zip instructed. "We'll run on the outside to protect you!"

"But what about Shlep?" Becky shouted.

"Everyone together, run east!" Ice Z ordered.

"But they'll get Shlep!" Becky protested. The monkey had run in the opposite direction, to the west.

"Go!" Ice Z commanded. "Run! Run! Run!"

The herd took off to the east in a frenzy of pounding hoofbeats and flying dust.

But Becky didn't run east with them. She ran west, after Shlep.

Directly toward the approaching lions.

CHAPTER TWENTY-FIVE

Home

MRS. ZASLOW SAT in the living room, slowly rocking in the old rocking chair. It had been her great-grandmother's passed down, mother to daughter, for three generations. In it she had held Becky and Lee as babies, feeding them, singing to them, soothing away their hurts and bad dreams.

Mr. Zaslow looked out the picture window. "It's summer," he said. "That doesn't seem right."

The chair creaked as Mrs. Zaslow rocked. "Maybe we didn't do the right thing, bringing Becky home."

"She woke up, Diane. She came back to us. And she told us what she wanted."

Mrs. Zaslow kept rocking. "But just because the transplant didn't work doesn't mean we should give up. Maybe there's an experimental program—"

"There's nothing."

She put her hands over her heart as if she could stop it from breaking. "But we're her parents," she said. "We're supposed to protect her."

Her husband turned on her. "Don't you think I know that?" he exploded. "I'm a cop! I spend my life protecting people! How do you think it feels to know I can't protect my own little girl?"

"Daddy?" Lee came hesitantly into the doorway.

Her husband inhaled deeply, trying to calm himself. "What is it, son?"

"Was there something wrong with my bone marrow?"

"No, Lee, of course not," his father assured him.

"Then why is Becky . . . ?"

His father went to him and picked him up. "We don't know," he admitted, rubbing the little boy's back. "But it's not your fault."

Lee hugged his father as hard as he could. "Becky says she wants you to carry her into the living room now."

* * *

"EVERYONE, run with the herd!" Ice Z ordered as the herd fled from the lions.

"I can't keep up, go on without me!" Papa Zeke insisted. He was galloping as fast as he could, but it wasn't fast enough anymore.

"No matter what, we stay together!" Ice Z barked. He galloped around the outside of his herd and caught sight of the marauding lions in the distance, gaining on them. Papa Zeke *was* slowing them down. Still, Ice Z would not allow the herd to abandon him.

"I'm not risking my hide for that old zebra," Zilch bellowed. "It's every zebra for himself!" As the herd veered right, Zilch broke left, galloping away as fast as he could. He threw his head back and wildly *kwa*'d his independence into the wind.

Too late, he saw the termite mound directly ahead of him. Instinctively he took a flying leap over it. He missed, and crashed heavily into the mound. There was a loud crack as his right foreleg broke below the knee.

"Help!" he cried pitifully, rolling down the termite mound to the grass below. "Help!"

But the pounding hooves of the fleeing zebras made the earth shake. He couldn't possibly be heard. Panicked, Zilch sniffed the air, and his heart missed a beat.

He could smell the lions.

With the greatest of effort, he managed to stand. But his right leg collapsed instantly, and he fell back to the grass.

"He-e-elp!" he pleaded. "Someone save me!"

The lions roared. They had scented his fear. They were coming for him.

Zilch rolled onto his back, wailing piteously, and turned his throat up. At least it would be over quickly.

"Zilch!"

He opened his eyes. Standing over him was Becky, with Shlep clinging to her back.

"Save me!" Zilch pleaded.

"Why aren't you with the herd?" Becky asked.

"They got away! But I broke my leg and they heartlessly left me behind. The lions are coming. Please, you have to help me."

"Why should we?" Shlep asked.

"Because I'm a zebra!"

More roars as the lions drew nearer.

"Well, I'm a filthy little green *monkey*," Shlep replied. "Sorry."

"Then I'm doomed!" Zilch moaned.

"Guess so," Shlep agreed cheerfully. He jumped off Becky's back and took her hand. "See ya, Zilch, wouldn't wanna be ya."

Becky hung back. "Wait, Shlep. Maybe you're not a zebra. But that doesn't mean you can't be a hero."

Shlep pointed at his chest. "Me?"

"Yes, you, please," Zilch implored. "They're coming!"

"Think, Shlep," Becky urged as she helped get Zilch up on his four legs. "What could a heroic monkey do to save a zebra's life? Something that a zebra could never do?"

Shlep thought hard. He couldn't run as fast or leap as far or—and then it came to him.

The lions roared and came over a rise in a dead run.

"Go!" the monkey screeched to Becky and Zilch. "Go!"

As Becky helped Zilch limp away, the little green monkey did something amazing. He ran toward the lions, jumping up and down to catch their attention, making his loudest, most appalling monkey noises.

The lions stopped, puzzled, twenty feet from the monkey. What was this? Their eyes gleamed and saliva dripped from their jaws.

Shlep screeched even louder. He scratched his armpits. He walked on his hands, then did a back flip. He pointed at the lions and laughed at them, beating his chest.

With a horrendous roar, they sprang at him.

Zoom! Shlep took off, his feet barely touching the

ground as he sprinted for the nearest tree. He leaped onto it and scrambled up to the highest branch as the attacking lions circled below, growling furiously.

"I did it!" Shlep cried. "I'm a hero!"

The lions roared again, and Shlep looked down into their open mouths, full of teeth that could catch a green monkey with one swift move and chew him to bits with the next.

"Uh, see, you guys can't climb this tree," Shlep told them cautiously. "So you might as well be going now."

The largest lion charged the acacia tree, trying to knock Shlep from it. The monkey held on as the tree shook.

"Becky?" he called nervously. "They're not leaving."

There was no answer from Becky, and the lions didn't leave. They formed a deadly circle around the tree.

"Nice kitties," Shlep cooed at them. "Shoo. Go away now. Go away. Please go away now. Go away . . ."

"GO AWAY," Becky whispered hoarsely as her father carried her into the living room. "Go away now. Go away." He put Becky in her mother's arms in the rocking chair.

"Who's she talking to?" Lee asked.

"I don't know," his father said. He put one arm around his son as he held his daughter's hand.

Becky opened her eyes. "Daddy?"

"I'm right here, Becks."

"I don't want the lions to get Shlep. Mom?"

"Yes, baby?" her mother whispered.

"You have to take care of Daddy."

"We'll all take care of each other," her mother promised her. "You and Lee and—"

"I don't want to leave you," Becky whispered, "but—"

Mrs. Zaslow felt her husband's hand on her shoulder. "She won't go until you tell her it's okay, Diane," he said softly.

"But we can't give up," she said. "We can't."

"We're not giving up," he gently told her. "We're setting her free."

Slowly Mrs. Zaslow began to rock Becky in her arms. She put her mouth down to her daughter's ear, and her voice was the barest, sweetest whisper.

> *Hush, my darling, don't fear, my darling,*
> *the lion sleeps tonight.*
> *Hush, my darling, don't fear, my darling,*
> *the lion sleeps tonight.*

Becky gazed up at Lee and handed him her stuffed zebra. "Don't be sad. I'll always be with you."

"It's okay to go now, Becky," her mother told her as she rocked her child in her arms.

"You're not alone, Becky," Mr. Zaslow said. "You'll never be alone."

Now Becky's mother and brother added their voices. "You'll never be alone," they all said. "You'll never be alone. You'll never be alone. . . ."

In a place far, far away, the voice of a very, very old zebra joined in.

You'll never be alone, Becky. You'll never be alone. If you can show such true courage, then so can this old zebra.

Though exhausted by his flight from the lions, the oldest zebra in all of Africa began to walk, then trot, then gallop as he had not galloped in many years. Then, with the mightiest of efforts, he concentrated all his feelings, his imagination, and his spirit, leaped into the air, shimmered between the beats of his heart, and was gone.

Becky opened her eyes.

She knew.

Papa Zeke stood next to her mother's rocking chair, his rheumy eyes full of love. Becky smiled at him. She stood up. It was so easy. She climbed onto his back and wrapped her arms around his neck. Then she looked back at her family rocking her, singing her, loving her into another place.

They'll always be with me, Papa Zeke. Even when I'm somewhere else. Just like you were always with me here.

Exactly. Are you ready?

She nodded peacefully. She was going home.

CHAPTER TWENTY-SIX

True Courage

". . . AND THEN I did what a zebra could never do—monkeyshines!" Shlep told the enthralled herd. "So that the lions would come after me instead of Zilch."

"You saved Zilch's life?" Zuzi asked incredulously. "On *purpose*?"

"Of course on purpose," Zilch said crossly, limping over to join them.

"Well, you didn't deserve it," Zuzi declared.

"Did too," Zilch insisted.

"Did not," Zuzi jeered. "Did not, did not, did—"

"Enough already!" Papa Zeke growled. He was so weak that he leaned against a baobab tree for support.

"Shlep, you're our hero," Zip and Zap said together, and the two mares slurped him with sloppy zebra kisses. The monkey grinned wildly.

"Were you very scared?" Zuzi asked.

"Nah, I was plucky," Shlep boasted. "There were about a hundred lions, too. No, a thousand. *More* than a thousand. But I gave 'em my right paw. And then my left. And then I—"

"Climbed a tree," Zilch said dryly. "That's how you saved me. All you did was climb a tree."

Shlep folded his arms. "So? I didn't see *you* climb a tree to save yourself, mister." The whole herd laughed, and Shlep went on. "You see, what happened was, Becky asked me 'what could a heroic monkey do to—'"

He stopped suddenly. "Hey. Where's Becky?"

The herd looked this way and that, murmuring uneasily. Becky was nowhere to be seen. Finally Ice Z turned to Papa Zeke. "Please tell us she went back to the human world," he implored.

Papa Zeke didn't reply. He only blinked slowly.

"But she has to be okay," the monkey said. "She's my best friend."

"She's our human," the herd said sadly.

It was a long time before Papa Zeke finally spoke. "Becky had a very bad sickness, my zebra children. She had courage. She fought right up until the end."

"No!" Shlep cried, throwing his paws over his eyes.

"I don't understand," Zip said.

"Me neither," said Zap.

"Papa Zeke?" Ice Z asked, and there was a hurt edge to his voice. "If we're part of Becky, and she's—she's gone . . . how can we still be here?"

Papa Zeke let his eyes sweep from zebra to zebra, taking in the entire herd. "How many times have I told you, my zebra children? A person is not her body. A person is—"

Shlep stepped forward. "A person is . . . her feelings?" he asked tentatively.

The old zebra nodded.

Ice Z lifted his head. "A person is her imagination," he recalled.

"Exactly," Papa Zeke agreed.

"And a person is—" the herd began.

They were all startled by the sound of thundering hooves in the distance. A plume of dust rose as the hoofbeats grew louder, then louder still. A powerful creature was coming, but they could not see it for the whirling dust. Then they heard a mighty "Kwa!" as the charging animal launched itself skyward in a tremendous leap, high above the savanna.

A splendiferous, multicolored, polka-dotted zebra landed in front of them.

"And a person is her spirit!" said the beautiful zebra, its voice ringing out over the savanna.

"Becky!" Shlep ran to the polka-dotted zebra and jumped on its back, hugging it with all his monkey might.

"But that's not Becky," Zuzi said, her voice awestruck. "That's . . . Zink!"

Ice Z's eyes shone. "Yes. The bravest zebra, with the most courage—"

"—and the biggest heart," Zip and Zap said.

"Zink the zebra!" the herd cheered.

Zilch fell to the ground and crawled on his belly toward the polka-dotted zebra. "All hail, Your Zinkness. Your Highness, Your Polka-dottedness—"

"Oh, Zilch, get up," Zink told him, and her voice was Becky's. "You're getting your hide all dirty. I know how much you hate that."

Zilch struggled up. "But you're Zink the zebra, and I am but a lowly—"

"I'm Zink, *a* zebra. Not Zink *the* zebra."

"And you're Becky, too," Shlep said happily, hugging her neck again. "My best friend."

Zink nodded. "I'm the same as all of you. I just look a little different. A zebra isn't her body any more than a person is her body. Or a monkey, for that matter."

Shlep jumped off Zink's back. "I knew that," he said.

Zink walked regally over to Papa Zeke. "Hello, old friend," she greeted him softly.

Papa Zeke licked a blade of star grass from his upper lip. "Good to see you," he replied. "You're looking well. You put on a little weight, maybe. Nice dots."

"Did you know I was Zink all along, Papa Zeke?"

"The answer to your question is . . ."

The whole herd waited. This time, just maybe . . .

"I don't know," Papa Zeke concluded.

The herd groaned.

"However," the old zebra went on, "in my opinion, you make a heck of a Zink."

The herd agreed loudly, until Zilch's voice rose above the others.

"Just a mo', Zink, Becky, whatever you say your name is," he said derisively. "Do you mean to tell us there's nothing special about you? Nothing remotely godlike?"

"Nothing," Zink said.

"But this is preposterous," Zilch sputtered. "Our human turns out to be Zink, but Zink turns out to be a funny-looking nothing!"

"You're the nothing, Zilch. That's why I hate you," Zuzi spat. "Everyone hates you!"

"Don't yell at him," little Zero retorted, kicking Zuzi's foreleg.

The whole herd began to squabble, nostrils flaring, hooves flying. Papa Zeke ignored them, lowering his head to bite off a blade of star grass he'd missed earlier.

"Please stop," Zink said softly. No one heard her.

She tried again. No one listened.

Finally she reared up and *kwa*'d more loudly than any zebra had ever *kwa*'d before.

Startled, the herd hushed.

Zink turned to Papa Zeke. "Once and for all, you have to tell me why they won't stop fighting," she insisted.

Papa Zeke gummed some more grass.

"You're the oldest and wisest," Zink went on, her frustration rising. "You're supposed to know. *Someone has to know!*"

"Exactly," Papa Zeke said emphatically. "Now we're getting somewhere, I agree. But who that someone is . . ."

"Don't tell me," Zink sighed. "You don't know."

"Not exactly," Papa Zeke said.

The herd gasped in shock. Had they heard right?

"You mean you *do* know?" Zink asked.

"Not everything, but something," Papa Zeke admitted.

Zink and the entire herd waited, perfectly still.

"The something I know is this," Papa Zeke said. "Zebras fight because they don't dare think about which zebra the lions will kill next." He regarded Zink closely. "Do *you* know which zebra that will be?"

Zink looked from zebra to zebra to zebra. It could be any of them.

It could even be her.

"No," she finally admitted softly.

"Neither do they." Papa Zeke shrugged. "No one knows. Not even me."

Zink thought for a moment. "I think I understand," she said slowly. "There are terrible predators everywhere. Perfectly nice kids get sick and die for no reason. And perfectly nice zebras get eaten by lions—"

"—for no reason," Ice Z finished. "I can't protect them all."

Zink nodded. "Once when I was very scared, my friend taught me the meaning of true courage." Her eyes met Ice Z's. "True courage is admitting we're afraid and fighting the predators anyway."

Her eyes swept over the herd. "Fighting *them*," she said. "Not fighting each *other*."

All the zebras glared at Zilch.

"Though it pains me to admit it," Zilch said grudgingly, "Zink is correct."

"Thank you," Zuzi said.

"Which is why you should all stop fighting with me," Zilch added quickly.

"Zilch!" Zink chided him.

Zilch groaned. "Oh, all right," he muttered. "And I should stop fighting with all of you."

"Exactly!" Papa Zeke said. As the herd *kwa*'d its agreement, he turned to Zink. "So our Zink is a zebra philosopher with dots. Who knew? Just one thing I would add. Fighting is a bad way to fill your head so that you won't be afraid. But there are good ways. Jokes are good. Stories are also good."

"And singing!" the Z'bras sang out in three-part harmony.

"And singing," Papa Zeke approved.

Heads together, Zip and Zap began to chant.

Wimoweh, a-wimoweh, a-wimoweh, a-wimoweh . . .

The beat was infectious, and one by one, the rest of the herd joined in.

Wimoweh, a-wimoweh, a-wimoweh, a-wimoweh . . .

Zink touched her nose to Papa Zeke's and a strange and wonderful electricity filled the air. The Serengeti sky flashed from blue to purple to the brightest pink, as all the zebras chanted and swayed together.

Wimoweh, a-wimoweh, a-wimoweh, a-wimoweh . . .

Then Zink opened her mouth, and with all of her feelings, her imagination, and her spirit, she began to sing.

In the jungle, the mighty jungle, the lion sleeps tonight.
In the jungle, the mighty jungle, the lion sleeps tonight.
Hush, my darling, don't fear, my darling, the lion sleeps
   tonight.
Hush, my darling, don't fear, my darling, the lion sleeps
   tonight!

Epilogue

LEE SLAMMED into the house, stomped up to his room, and dived onto his bed.

Just as she had every afternoon since second grade had started a week before, his mom had met his bus after school. Today he'd silently handed her the note from his teacher, who had already told him what it said.

> Lee refuses to read in class. Please call me to
> set up an appointment so that we can discuss
> how to help him.
>
> *Francine Appell*

When his mom had read it, she had gotten very upset. And of course she'd wanted to talk about it right away, because that therapist lady they had all seen after Becky died told them they needed to talk to each other more.

"Why won't you read?" his mother had asked him. "Are you mad, or sad? Is it about Becky?"

That was when Lee took off ahead of his mom. He didn't care what anyone said. He didn't want to talk about it, he wasn't going to talk about it, and no one could make him talk about it. It was a secret between him and his sister.

I told Becky only she could help me with my reading, he recalled. *Well, Mom told her for me. But it was still a promise.*

It made perfect sense to him. If Becky couldn't help him, he wasn't going to read. Ever. It was the least he could do to make up for the bad thing he'd said to her in Florida, about how he should have pretended to have had cancer so people would feel sorry for him and let him go on the world's biggest water slide.

There was a knock on his door. "Lee?" his mom called.

"Go away."

"We don't have to talk about it right now," his mom said through the door, "but we do have to talk about it later, when Dad gets home. Do you want a snack?"

"No."

"I'll be downstairs if you change your mind."

As soon as he heard his mom walk away, he went to the door and opened it a crack. Good. She was gone. He hurried down the hall and opened another door, the one that was always closed, and went inside.

Becky's room still looked exactly the same. His parents said they weren't ready to change it yet, and Lee was glad. He liked to go in there. Sometimes he even slept in her bed.

He lay down on it now, holding the scruffy stuffed zebra, the one she'd given him, on one raised knee.

"I hate this kid in my class, Bruce," he said, making the zebra do a high dive onto his stomach. "He laughs at me because I won't read and tells everyone it's because I don't know how. He's so mean."

Lee got up and wandered around the room. Sometimes touching Becky's things made him feel better. He pulled a big box out of her closet. It was full of Becky's stuff, which his parents had brought home from the hospital. He'd never looked all the way through it before. He sat in front of the box.

Right on top was the blue ribbon he'd made for her. BEKCY IS #1. YU DU NOT LIP-STINK. The circle of sticky-tape was still on the back, and he pressed the ribbon to his chest. He dug deeper. Books and more books. Books recorded on cassettes. More books. Lots of get-well cards, including some from him.

Under it all was Becky's box of music cassettes.

Lee took them out and looked through them. Superhero Sam and the Space Bandits Band. Boy, he sure had been a baby when he'd given that tape to her. What else? Tapes from Becky's classmates at school. More books on cassettes. "The Lion Sleeps Tonight"— the tape with Becky's favorite song. Lee decided he'd listen to it so that he could learn the song too.

Under all the tapes, he found her cassette player. There was already a tape in it.

A tape marked LEE, in the wobbly scrawl Becky had used after she'd gotten really sick.

His face got all hot and his breathing felt funny.

It was a tape for him.

He looked at the little buttons on the cassette player. He pressed the On button.

Nothing happened. The tape was blank.

Then Becky's voice filled the air.

Hi, Lee, it's me. Hey, that rhymes! Well, I wanted to tell you how much I love the blue ribbon you made for me. It's even better than if I really had won by singing the best. No, wait. That's a lie. Um . . . it's even better in a different way than if I really had won. That's better. There's all this stuff I want to tell you but I don't know if I'll get the chance. I know you always say you're not afraid of anything, but I just wanted to say that it's okay to be afraid. What's really brave is to admit you're afraid and then to try your best anyway. I need to learn that one myself, I think! There's so much more, but . . . I'll tell you when I see you. But just in case I can't, I have something for you. It's my secret journal and you are the only one who is allowed to read it. You have to read the whole thing by yourself, though, no help. After that, if you want to read it to Mom and Dad, you can. So . . . I'm kind of tired now and Angela has to take my temperature. Oh, she says hi. Well, I'll tape more later maybe. So good night, sleep tight, don't let the sweat bees sting. That's a joke you'll get after you read my journal. . . . Oh, start reading on page sixty-three, okay? After you finish, you can go back and read the happy stuff from before I got sick so you can remember all the good times we had together. And remember, you have to read it all yourself. Oh, one last thing, Lee. Africa is the most wonderful place.

Lee kept listening, but the rest of the tape was blank. He looked inside the box again, pushing aside all the get-well letters. And there, at the very bottom, in a separate box, on top of some other tapes, was Becky's secret journal.

He took it out and opened it. There were tiny page numbers on the bottom of each page. What page was it she'd said to start on again? Sixty-three.

Lee peered at Becky's neat printing.

"Sep . . . Sep-tem . . . September," he read aloud. "September 28. To-day I am an Af . . . A-fer. No, A-*free* . . . African. Prin-cess. Today I am an African princess!"

As the late-afternoon sun began to fade and the sky changed from blue to purple to the brightest pink, Lee discovered how much he could love to read.

AFTERWORD

by Bruce M. Camitta, M.D., Rebecca Jean Slye Professor of Pediatric Oncology and director of the Midwest Children's Cancer Center, Medical College of Wisconsin and Children's Hospital of Wisconsin, Milwaukee

Acute lymphocytic leukemia (ALL) is a cancer of the body's blood-forming factory, the bone marrow. Only rarely is ALL caused by inherited factors. In most cases, the illness is the result of an acquired change in the genetic material of a single bone marrow cell (blast). This change enables the blast to continually divide, producing more of itself instead of growing up to be a mature cell (lymphocyte). As abnormal blasts fill up the normal bone marrow, there is no room to produce normal blood cells. This results in tiredness (due to anemia, a lack of red blood cells, which carry oxygen), fever (due to a lack of white blood cells, which fight infection), and bleeding (due to lack of platelets, which help blood clot). Eventually, when the bone marrow is full, the blasts spill into the blood and travel through the body, causing many other symptoms. When leukemia is diagnosed in an individual, there are about one *trillion* leukemia cells in his or her body.

Cancer is rare in children; only one person in six hundred will develop cancer before his or her fifteenth birthday. Leukemias are the most common form of childhood cancer. ALL accounts for eighty percent of all leukemias in children.

Seventy-five percent of children with ALL are cured with drugs (chemotherapy) specially designed to kill leukemia cells. These medicines are given by mouth, or by injections into muscles, into veins, or into the fluid that bathes the brain and spinal cord. Many patients develop unwanted, but usually temporary, side effects from chemotherapy.

In some children, leukemia recurs despite initial chemotherapy. Recurrent leukemia is more difficult to treat. Some children can be cured by more chemotherapy using different drugs. More recently, bone marrow transplantation (BMT) has been able to cure almost fifty percent of children who relapse. Before a BMT, a patient receives very high doses of chemotherapy or irradiation (or both) to kill most of the leukemia cells in the body. Normal bone marrow cells are also killed but are then replaced by healthy bone marrow from a related or unrelated donor with the same tissue type (HLA type). Any two children with the same parents have a twenty-five percent chance of having the same type.

The beautifully crafted, sensitive story in this book presents a plausible, although fortunately not typical, scenario for childhood ALL. However, beyond the medical facts, several other important themes are dealt with: honesty, teamwork, bravery, and friendship.

Children need to be told honestly what is happening to them. Explanations should be tailored to the child's age and developmental and intellectual abilities. It is a mistake to think that children can be shielded from fears (real or imagined) by keeping them isolated from the facts. As Becky demonstrates, kids being treated for cancer will learn the facts anyway. Becky might have benefited from more openness from her parents on many occasions—from diagnosis until her death. Even with the most loving parents, fear can make this more easily said than done.

Leukemia is an illness that occurs in the context of an individual's life. To best treat the disease, the medical team must work in concert with the child's family and other support systems.

Bravery is not the absence of fear. Rather, it is the ability to act in a purposeful fashion in spite of being scared. To do this, we may draw upon internal resources: our past experiences or our fantasy world (our zebras). Equally important are external resources, such as friends. A child with a serious illness often views himself or herself as different—maybe even as a zebra with polka dots like Zink. Acceptance by peers, despite the difference of cancer, holds out hope that if and when the leukemia is eradicated, the child really can resume a normal life.

And hope is what battling a potentially fatal illness is all about.

Prologue

Alicia O'Brien, age 13,
lives in Illinois. She is battling brain
cancer. Alicia loves theater, music,
art, and using her imagination.

Chapter 2

Nechemia Farkas, age 11,
lives in Brooklyn, New York.
Nechemia's brother Shalam died
of leukemia. Nechemia enjoys all
sports, especially basketball,
baseball, hockey, and in-line skating.
He likes to read mysteries.

Chapter 5

Anna Daoud, age 14, lives in Rome, Georgia. She is battling cancer and as of March 1999 has only one more month of chemotherapy to go. Anna enjoys playing basketball, swimming, and football.

Chapter 7

(photograph not
available)

Alice Livermore, age 11, lives in
Westbury, New York. She is in
remission from ALL-type leukemia.
Alice enjoys sports,
reading, and drawing.
Her favorite color is yellow.

Chapter 8

Rochel Steinhaus, age 14,
lives in Brooklyn, New York.
Her brother died from leukemia.
She enjoys drawing, reading,
and writing.

Chapter 11

Jenna Paige Leitman, age 12, lives in Roslyn Heights, New York. She has survived leukemia. She enjoys acting, dancing, singing, playing with her dog, Mariah, and going to sleepaway camp.

Chapter 16

Cinthia Mora, age 15, lives in
Atlanta, Georgia. She is in
remission from leukemia. Cinthia likes
to draw, play on the computer,
swim, bowl, go to school,
go shopping, and go to the movies.

Chapter 21

A. J. Wheeler, age 11, lives in
Merton, Wisconsin. He has been
diagnosed with acute lymphocytic
leukemia. A.J. enjoys sketching,
football, and video games.

Chapter 22

Cheri Amore, age 13, lives in Twin Lakes, Wisconsin. She is currently in remission from ALL/AML, after BMT in 1996. Cheri enjoys water-skiing, downhill skiing, and dancing. She plays piano and clarinet. Her best friend is Elliott, a Dalmatian.

A Swahili Glossary

PREPARED WITH THE ASSISTANCE OF DR. DONATH
MRAWIRA AND DR. HASSAN ALI

*Swahili is spoken by more than fifty million people, principally in
Kenya, Tanzania, and Uganda, but also elsewhere in East Africa.
Swahili words are generally pronounced with an equal accent on each
syllable.*

asante (AH-SON-TAY) Thank you.

Dar es Salaam (DAR ES SAH-LAHM) Haven of peace.
Tanzania's biggest city and capital.

kanga (KAHN-GAH) A colorful wrapped garment worn by
women.

Kila jambo na wakati wake (KEY-LA JAM-BOW NAH WAH-KAH-TEE WAH-KAY) There is a time for everything.

machoni rafiki, moyoni mnafiki MAH-TCHO-NEE RAH-FEE-KEY, MOW-YO-NEE MMM-NAH-FEE-KEY) Friendly in the eyes, a hypocrite in the heart.

msichana (MMM-SEE-TCHAH-NAH) Little girl.

mwalimu (MMWAH-LEE-MOO) Teacher.

punda milia (POON-DAH MEE-LEE-YAH) Zebra.

rafiki (RAH-FEE-KEY) Friend.

ugali (OOH-GAH-LEE) The Tanzanian national dish, made of ground corn flour cooked with water until it becomes as stiff as mashed potatoes; normally served with beans or stew.

Usipokifata, hutakipata (OOO-SEE-POE-KEE-FAH-TAH, HOO-TAH-KEE-PAH-TAH) If you don't reach, you're never going to grab what you're after.

Usisafirie nyota ya mwenzio (OOH-SEE-SAH-FEE-REE-YEAH N'YOW-TAH YAH MWEN-ZEE-OH) Don't set sail using someone else's star.

About the Author

CHERIE BENNETT writes often on teen themes. Her 1998 Delacorte novel, *Life in the Fat Lane,* was one of the year's most talked-about books and was selected as an ALA Best Book for Young Adults. This novel, *Zink,* was adapted from her published play of the same title; her other published plays for young audiences include *Anne Frank & Me* and recent Kennedy Center New Visions/New Voices award winners *Cyra and Rocky* and *Searching for David's Heart.* Cherie also writes *Hey, Cherie!,* a nationally syndicated teen advice column, for Copley News Service. She and her husband, author and producer Jeff Gottesfeld, live in Los Angeles and Nashville. Cherie Bennett can be contacted at P.O. Box 150326, Nashville, Tennessee 37215, and by e-mail at authorchik@aol.com.